PANTHEON MAGAZINE

Vancouver, WA

Inset Layout and Design by Bailey Hunter
www.facebook.com/BaileyHunterDesign

Story illustrations © 2019 by Luke Spooner
www.carrionhouse.com

Cover Art © 2019 by Daniele Serra
www.danieleserra.com

Edited by Sarah Read

Published in the United States of America

For information about the authors, bios, and more, visit our site at:
www.pantheonmag.com

TABLE OF CONTENTS

TABLE OF CONTENTS

EDITOR'S NOTE

Many myths are stories of transformation, of emergence. The beginnings of new things—new creatures, new eras, new adventures. In myth, transformation can be empowering or punishing. A curse, or an ascendancy to great power—or both. Collected here are new myths, new stories of transformation—the emergence of some of the best new voices in genre fiction. Enjoy, and be changed.

-Sarah Read

WHO ARE YOU?

by Filip Wiltgren

At the first gate, you're asked for ten memories.

"Are these the ones I get to keep?" you ask the guard, already worrying about your piano lessons, and that time your entire family gathered to cook saffron rice.

"No," the guard says.

So you give them the time you peed yourself in third grade, your mother's cancer, and Mr. Winsler, your gymnastics coach. You give them all of Mr Winsler. When you leave the first gate, your steps are light.

"Who are you?" you're asked at the second gate.

You tell them your name, and give them the time you set fire to your aunt's tablecloth and blamed your cousin.

You leave the second gate smiling. After the third gate, you're laughing.

By the tenth, you're worried. You can't remember why. You give away a day at the office.

"Who are you?" You say your name. You give away a flat tire on a road trip you took in college. You give away a gray sky, the smell of a dumpster, running a red light.

You give away.

An argument, an ice-cold pool, a dropped cupcake. Your grandmother's kitchen, the color purple, the smell of pine trees in the evening.

You give away your mother cooking saffron rice, your father putting up your swing. You give away your brother, a day at the beach, that time you won the championship.

You give away your house, your pet, your childhood teddy.

"Who are you?" You give away your name.

"I don't know," you say.

You're dancing with your spouse at your wedding day. There is no sound. There is no smell. You give away your spouse's name, and dance with a stranger on your wedding day. You give away.

Your child's birth, laugh, cry. The school years, the later years.

You're holding your child in the middle of a meadow yellow with dandelions. You have cooked saffron rice together, for the first time. You give away the kitchen, the pot, the rice. You give away the dandelions, one after one. You give away the meadow, then your child's clothes, hair, hug, name.

You reach the final gate. Your arms are empty. Only the faint smell of saffron rice clings to you.

"Who are you?" you're asked.

"Saffron rice," you say, and walk into the light.

THE FACE GOD GAVE

by J. Ashley Smith

They were somewhere between LAX and Sydney, way out over the Pacific Ocean, when the plane hit rough air. The boys were both asleep, finally, and Karen lay in a waking doze, drained of all energy yet too wired to submit to sleep.

It was a relief to see them unconscious. They'd been awake so long, passed through so many time zones, that both boys had lost it completely. They had become so feral that even the endless loop of movies and TV no longer subdued them. But now Dylan was curled beside her with his head in her lap, snuggled under the airline blanket, one small, sock-less foot poking out from beneath. Torin lay rigid as a plank, mouth wide, with his head against the window-blind. The arm of Karen's seat was up and dug painfully into her shoulder with the sudden dip and shudder of the plane.

Karen had never before confessed this to herself, but she was terrified of flying. For the sake of the boys, she had pressed down her true feelings, wore a brave expression she hoped concealed how tightly she gripped the armrest as the plane peeled from the runway, how her belly churned each time, as now, they hit a bad patch of turbulence.

Her TV screen showed a pixellated map of their location. The plane icon was hemmed in by rippled shades of blue, uninterrupted by any green hieroglyphs of scattered islands or archipelagos. There was nothing beneath them but air; and, beneath that, only water. Karen forced herself to breathe slow and deep, suppressing the panic that tugged at her insides, that forced her to picture each of the ten-or-more-thousand metres between the plane and the ocean. The limitless void of black waves. The chill, fathomless depths.

The plane shook again and Karen felt her stomach drop, the sickening feeling of weightlessness. She clenched her fists, counted backwards from ten. The cabin was dimmed for night-time and, apart from the few insomniacs with their glimmering screens, most of the passengers were slumped beneath cheap blankets and eye-shades in restless sleep. No one but Karen seemed concerned by the lurching, rolling motions of the plane.

Something changed in the movements then. Something sudden and sick-making.

The plane banked hard to the right and the cabin tilted sharply down. Bags slid out from under seats. Untethered headphones skittered down the aisle. Torin's head bumped the window-blind and he woke with a jerk, yanked off his eye-shade, searching for Karen. She reached out to comfort him, but even that small movement almost pulled her from the seat. She gripped the outside armrest, clutched at the stirring Dylan with her free hand, looked to Torin with eyes she hoped betrayed none of her panic.

They were dropping, the plane in a mad spin. Karen couldn't see it, but she could feel it, in her guts, in her madly popping ears. People were waking now, yelling, trying to stand but pulled back into their seats by the plane's relentless drag. A voice squelched over the Tannoy, words lost in the din from whining engines, from frightened passengers. A businessman across from Karen forced himself from his seat to open an overhead locker. Cases tumbled into the cabin, banged off seats, clattered down the aisle. One struck the man and knocked him to the floor. People were screaming. The captain had switched on the fasten seatbelts sign.

There was a gasping sound then, a deep hissing sigh, and masks dropped from the ceiling.

Karen struggled to remember the brace position, the location of the emergency exits, how to find and deploy her lifejacket. But her mind was a blank. Throughout the safety demonstration she had been wracked with shame and anxiety as Dylan kicked the seat in front and Torin badgered her without cease about some game he wanted her to buy. She had felt the eyes of the other passengers, of the cabin crew, burning into her: the bad mother. Now she wished she had ignored the children, ignored her self-reproach, paid attention instead to the formalised ritual of the cabin crew's safety display, to the comforting infographics of the flight safety card.

She reached for the dropped masks and Dylan gripped her arm, buried his face into her belly. Torin clutched at the seat, his face stretched and pale with terror. But when her fingers found the edge of the mask, Karen recoiled.

What she had pulled towards herself was not made of plastic, but of fur. Stiff and leathery, the feel was of something long dead, desiccated with age. It was the face of a fox.

There was a hissing sound and the cabin filled with thick white mist. The lights failed and the total darkness was broken only by a strobing exit sign. The plane was still falling, falling. Karen's breath came in stifled gasps. Beside her, Dylan wheezed and Torin scratched at his throat. Karen gripped the fox mask and pressed it onto her face.

The mask smelled of dried meat and ancient taxidermy, with a faint but unmistakable tang of musk. Yet it did not repel her, as she had expected. It was, in fact, oddly comforting. She could breathe without effort. Her night vision had improved.

She reached for another, saw Torin doing the same. The mask she pulled over Dylan's face was dark brown, with round ears and a snub nose. A bear. Torin, when she turned to him, looked back at her through the eyes of a young stag, the twin forks of antlers jutting from the back of his head. All around them, passengers were donning their own masks. Faces of geese, of badgers, of echidnas, bilbys and goannas. There were starlings, salamanders, pigs and toads and tigers. There were lemurs and lions, all manner of creatures, many Karen had no names for.

But there was no impact.

One moment, the plane was plummeting in a desperate, twisting, terminal dive. And the next...

Stillness. Silence. The dark.

All along the aisle, tiny lights fired one after another, illuminating a path to the exit doors. Looking closer, Karen saw they were glow-worms.

Passengers slipped from their seats and followed the lights. Not in the chaos of panic, but in a respectful, orderly procession. Some padded on paws, others trotted on hooves, others scratched at the carpet with claws. Some frisked and flittered from seat-back to seat-back. As Karen guided the boys into the aisle, she too felt the change, the acuteness of her sense of smell, the way she turned to lick Dylan as he rolled out of his seat. By the time Torin clopped past, she no longer thought of him by his name, but by the complex grammar of odours that poured from his tautly muscular body.

Daylight poured in from a hole in the side of the plane. The emergency exit door had been fired and a gazelle, still wearing the hat and scarf of the cabin crew, was guiding the procession out and down. Torin nuzzled her as he passed, reared and snorted, before stumbling down the rubbery yellow slide.

Karen nudged Dylan with her snout, persuading him with gentle motions onto and over the lip of the inflatable slide. As he spilled, slipping and rolling towards the jungle floor, he looked up at Karen with round eyes full of desperation and loss. But by the time he reached the bottom, the look had faded and he turned from the slide without pause to carve his own path, following the slowly dispersing crowd of animal passengers. Torin had already vanished into the living green.

The smells that came to Karen were rich and alive, danced in her nostrils like scent poems. From deep within the boundless jungle, sounds came to her, unfamiliar calls, the cries of unseen birds. The weight in her breast was already lightening, and lifted entirely as she stepped forward onto the slide. When her paws connected with the moist ground, tangled as it was with vines and the roots of vast fig trees, there was nothing left of Karen but the lightness.

She followed her sons into the understory of that first and final garden.

UNDONE

by Richard Thomas

...and when we turn off into the woods I know it's a mistake, abandoning the road, the highway that has stretched out into the darkness for days now, the sun a distant memory, even though there has been nothing in the rear view mirror for miles, for hours, that choice is what makes all the difference, what cements our demise, Xina, and I, a couple for only as long as the night spilled across the land, for as long as the rest of our kind disappeared, and they filled in every inch of our existence in winged flocks that scattered and remade themselves, in the water where they schooled and wove between all other swimming creatures, in the earth where they burrowed deep into the dirt and soil, and then the corners of every room, every frame, shadows that spilled and expanded, never quite in our line of sight, but never quite gone either, Xina, with her red hair that fanned out behind her like flames, Xina, with her piercing green eyes that shifted from jealousy to panic to fear to survival, Xina, as she tumbled from the car door, smoke unfurling out of the hood, something ticking from under the metal frame, the Nova getting us so far from everything, and yet, not really buying us much time at all, not *really*, her door popping open first and mine second, a cloud of dust filling our lungs as the dirt road and gravel and weeds fill in around us, the end of the road, the fence there locked and chained, the forest looming up and out as the only place we might possibly find cover, the singular path between two ancient oak trees that bend toward each other, as Xina and I seek each other out in our frantic loping toward the foliage, glancing back, but nothing quite yet appearing—but soon, we know, soon—so we keep going, and as we grasp for each other, off into the trees, Xina trips and falls, and a sweat of panic washes over me as her swollen belly distends, her arms outstretched, hands that have nails bitten to the quick, no longer in my grasp, nothing I can do now but watch, and breathe, my heart hammering my rib cage, her scream something we should not release into the night, but her reaction is one of instinct, trying to brace her fall, and when I realize that she's going to lose the baby, when I glance back and see a scattering of leather wings across the night, flicking moonlight into the air, a fluttering rising up to drown out her cries, I know I have to keep going, and she knows it too, sobbing into the dirt, hands to her stomach, and below that, between her legs, her eyes wide, as I smell the blood, and it's just the one nod she gives me— my name muttered for perhaps the last time ever, *Malaki*—but it's enough for me to not even slow my pace but instead quicken it, leaping over her as I whisper how sorry I am, as I cry out to her asking for forgiveness, as the smell of something foul fills the space between her and I and them—I keep moving, a stitch in my side, a tightness in my chest, because she's not the only one that's pregnant, not the only host here, and that's something else entirely that keeps bubbling up to the surface, one layer of tension the way that she might give birth in the woods, or a stream, or the back of the car, but another entirely different swelling of alarm the way that I will bring my child into the world, no obvious way for it to happen, not built for this, the agreement we made months ago something that was noble and obvious and not even up for debate until now, when I feel the kick, when I feel the bile rising, once more glancing back, this time to the ground cracking, and something slithering out in waves, and I'm into the trees, no longer going to look back, because I'm *it*, the last one, and it won't be long now, one way or the other, so I run, eyes on the path, slashes of pale moonlight splitting the forest in dazzling motes and beams of diminishing hope, moving forward, not familiar with this part of the state, this part of the country, but the smell of something musty in the air, as a cool breeze pushes through the bending trees, and I think water, maybe, it might be water, but I'm running so fast, breathing so hard, that it's hard to hear over my own desperate noises, my own gasping for air, heart rattling out a beat that has to slow, has to stop sometime soon, but not yet, not quite yet, and then I see it on the left, and then to the right, something pacing me in the trees, weaving in and out of the branches, the bushes, the cairns of rocks, and I curse the darkness, knowing I'm not nearly enough for this—up to it, capable, anything special at all—but if I can only hold on a bit longer, and my foot hits a root and I stumble, as it's *my* turn for my eyes to go wide, for my hands to push out bracing for the fall, but I right myself, and stagger up a hill, desperate to see the path, down another swell and the pain in my gut expands, something tearing, and I cry out, my silence no longer mattering really, as they close in, shadows and snapping branches, the sound of something heavy ripping out by the roots, a flash of white just caught for a moment to my right, the snapping of teeth, so long, and so sharp, the canopy of the forest rustling as something spills over the top of it all now, blocking out what little sick light was breaking through the leaves, and I can see now that the forest is coming to an end, it's a clearing up ahead, and that's not a good thing, out in the open, but I can go faster perhaps, if I don't simply split open before I get there, if my heart doesn't explode in a final fury, lungs withered in obsolescence, and then I hear it, what I thought I smelled before, water, something running fast and surely cold, the trees finally ending, as the field opens up, the tall grasses swaying back and forth as I fly into the open space, and across it, gnats and crickets leaping and spraying the air, and a handful of lightning bugs appear, causing me to clutch at my gut, to weep openly now as I continue to run—my knees burning, feet throbbing, arms covered in a slick sweat—no jar for me tonight, no tin foil and holes punched with a rusty screwdriver, and I laugh a harsh bark into the expanding gloom, unable to breathe or swallow, my insides twitching, and I only need to hold on a bit longer, to give my child a fighting chance here, as the grass cuts at my legs, risking one last look back, and that's a mistake, because they're here now, filling the space behind me, gaining, so close, and the only chance I have now is if what I heard, what I smell, is what I hope it is, not just water, but space and a bit more time, a few more seconds and then I see it—the end of the field, the water below rushing by, bellowing in its cold ambivalence, and I hit the edge of the cliff as their stench drifts to me, foul and rotten, something sour and spoiling, and then I leap into history as my flesh rips, and my child finally emerges, pushing out, splitting me open, and I help it to come into this world, already crying, both of us, as my hands, my fingers feel for the edge of the tear, pulling wider, opening the gap, and it is beautiful in its horror, everything I could never be, nothing we have been before—unfurling one appendage after the other, several wings flapping open, unfolding again and again, talons lost in the black of night, a gleam in its myriad of eyes, placed in a close cluster atop its elongated head, neck extending as its jaw unhinges, rows upon rows of teeth chattering in anticipation, and then the last of it comes free, the tail pulling out longer and longer, never seeming to end, the scales that cover it shimmering as the moon drifts out from behind a cluster of clouds, and I fall, knowing my work is done, but I'm wrong that my name was not uttered again, merely a different name this time, something I'd always longed to be, for it whispers my name, *Father*, as the rocks below rush up to me, the cold river undulating, the black mass descending, and when its wingspan fully unfurls, it blocks out the moon with an echoing finality.

PSALMS
by Aimee Ogden

The deer, who is not really a deer, flees.

Her heart beats frantic against the prison of her ribs. White froth rises in her mouth to choke her. She dares not slow, though, nor stop to rest. Else the man who loves her will find her again, and there are worse things he can cause her to be than merely cervine.

The man, the hunter, follows her through these dark woods. She hears his footsteps all around her, but maybe that is just the gallop of her heartbeat, or the echo of her hooves against the frozen ground. Her magic is older than his, but his is the stronger, and spellcraft flutters away from her on the deer's ragged breath. Perhaps he isn't everywhere at once, not really. But of course he doesn't need to be.

"My heart, my soul, my beauty." His voice shatters the icy moonlight that slices between bare trees, and the deer nearly loses her footing. The world is too wide around her through the deer's eyes, so large it crushes the air from her lungs. No, no, up again: there is no escape, no refusing to play the game. If she lies down at his feet and denies him the thrill of his chase, the stories they tell afterward will only say how much she wanted this. "I will hang your head in my hall, where men will sing your praises for centuries to come. You should be honored ..."

The deer does not want centuries of praise. She wants only this lifetime, the blood that rushes in her ears, the familiar contours and spaces of the body that used to be hers. There is no time left to wish for what has been taken, though. Now there is only the hope of denying the hunter the object of his appetite. Her hooves find purchase on a scrabble of dirt and her legs recoil for a sudden change of direction: saltation and exaltation. An arrow pierces the air where she would have been and strikes, quivering, in an oak tree. She mourns the ghost-self that would have died there, and she mourns the lost resolution of this chase as well.

Somewhere, everywhere, the hunter is laughing. Not in mockery, but in surprised awe. He loves her as the thirsting man loves the water, he tells her. His reverence is no smaller for its distortion.

The copse of trees falls away around her and she sees white light sliding over silver pelts before she recognizes her new companions. A cluster of forest deer, all does. Their tails flick up stark white at the speed of her passage—

She stops running.

They do not look up again when she returns to join them while they graze. Her heart still hammers in her ribcage but the little patch of winter grass is tender where it has slept beneath its blanket of snow. Another doe brushes up against her, flank to flank, and she meets golden-brown eyes. She musters what reserves of magic are left to her and listens to the shimmer of moonlight on snow, the warm swirl of misty breath. Yes. Perhaps.

She cannot take her own shape back. Not while he has anything to say about it. But she can, she thinks, press it upon another.

The arrow screams out a warning. Can you ever forgive me? she wants to ask the wide unblinking eyes of the doe. But she has no voice for the question, and the only answer to be had is the arrow's bite. The other doe's blood slashes the snow black. She stumbles to her knees as her herd panics and flees. Only the deer who is not really a deer stands and watches, and feels the earth tremble under his approach.

She makes the deer-shape cling to the other doe, several breaths past the moment when her rolling eyes still and her heaving sides quiet. She watches his face, drinks down that moment of doubt. His eyes shift upward—to her. The paean on his tongue thickens, threatening to curdle into something uglier.

Best not to linger. She changes the shape of the spell on the breath of an apology to the dead doe. Now she looks down into her own slack face. The hunter looks down too, and doubt and triumph war on the ancient canyons of his face.

His servants hurry forward to retrieve the cooling body. They disappear first into the night's shadows, but he stops to look back. At the black stain upon the snow, or the doe who did not flee.

She stares him down until at last he turns to follow the rest. Only then does she turn and pick her way over the tracks the herd has left. Let him wonder. Let him doubt the shape his arrow brought down. Let him gnaw forever on the bones of his denial. She will find her way back to her own shape again, or she will live and die as a creature of the forest. But she will not die as his creature. It is a small prize, less than she deserves. More, too. But it is hers. His doubt: the only vessel of immortality she needs.

She never asked for centuries of praise. But she has *survived*. And in that small way, at least, she has done something worthy of praise.

FIT FOR THE WOLVES

by Annie Neugebauer

When the goddess first lay down among the wolves, they did not eat her because she was pure.

They were not her creation, yet they were hers nonetheless—as she was theirs. At night they would lie in a warm pile of fur and skin and stare up at the strange white fruit that hung in the sky. When the fruit became ready they would lift their chins and howl for it, calling and begging and seducing with their song, yet the fruit never fell to the earth where they could reach it. No matter how many times the fruit ripened and rotted, disappearing to reseed before blossoming again, the goddess and her kin pined for a taste.

⌢

On this night, the fruit was budding but not yet full and round, and the wolves were growing hungry. If they could not taste the white flesh of the fruit, the goddess knew they must have other things to feed upon. So she drew herself up from their wet, sleepy breathing and their thick shaggy fur and the life-hardened pads of their big paws and she slunk barefoot into the forest.

It did not take long to find the hunter. He was a grizzled man whose dark beard surrounded a constant grin devoid of joy. It was not quite that he was baring his teeth, but it was not quite that he was smiling, either. With every movement he seemed to carry chagrin tucked beneath his clothes. Above his clothes, a long weapon leaned over his shoulder. The goddess could tell by his scent that he was not pure.

Here beneath the trees it was much darker than at the opening in front of the den, but the goddess knew he could see. The mortals did not have the eyes of her wolves, but they were not fully blind. She stepped on a twig to get his attention, then tread calmly past him. She walked from heel to toe, arms relaxed, hands down by her thighs, hips leading so her shoulders rested back in a way that made her breasts sway with each step. Her hair hung thick and heavy to her lower back.

The hunter turned.

The goddess ran. She did not have to look to know he'd follow. Her nudity was enough, with such as him. It always was.

She did not run fast. She knew these woods well, and the hunter was thick where she was thin, clumsy where she was grace, brutish where she was lithe, and she did not want to lose him. She slipped between branches and they closed behind her. He barreled through and snapped their spines.

By the time she made it back to the den, he sounded like a dying bear with snarling breath and steps that stomped the earth. The goddess ran right through the pile of wolves, waking them. The hunter stopped.

The largest of the nine, the wolf with the torn ear, rose and shook his mane. A look of confusion appeared on the hunter's face where the grin had been. The alpha's tongue glided over his teeth as the others stood.

The hunter had not fully turned before the wolves were upon him.

From behind her pack, the goddess watched.

⌒

When all of their muzzles were red and the hunter was gone, the wolves exposed their throats to the goddess and howled. She, too, lifted her face to the sky, staring at the strange white fruit that hung beyond reach. How she longed to taste it.

The goddess raised her voice and joined the supplication of the wolves.

It was not enough.

⌒

It was when the fruit had grown so ripe it was crisp near to bursting that the goddess next set out for food. She felt starved and restless, and though she did not partake in the pack's meals, she knew that hunting was the only thing that would bring her ease.

Yet she did not find a hunter. Nor a woodsman, nor a hermit, nor any other manner of mortal man who dwells in the forest.

She found the girl.

When the goddess saw her, she froze. The girl did not see her, so the goddess stood still beneath the trees and watched. It seemed the girl was whimpering.

She had shining hair that curled in heavy tendrils. Her limbs were long and soft, more untried than those of the goddess. Her body was fair of form but covered, and the goddess longed to know the shape hidden beneath her clothes. The skin that she could see was unblemished, paler than the bronzed goddess. Even from a distance, she smelled pure. The girl wept into her arms.

Shaking herself like one of the wolves, the goddess blinked. Her mouth filled with desire and her lip trembled, for she so desperately wished to call out. Instead, she carefully stepped on a twig.

The girl gasped, looking up at the sound. The goddess's heart pounded as she walked slowly by.

She looked over her shoulder, and her eyes met the girl's. They were wide and round, the same shape her lips formed. Would she follow?

The goddess ran.

The girl hesitated, so the goddess ran faster. It would be only moments before she disappeared between the trees.

Finally, letting out a lost, weak little cry, the girl gave chase.

⌒

The wolves would not have her.

Though she was wary of them at first, the girl was tired and afraid. Before long she lay down among the wolves, soft and white and full. She slept with her fingers buried in the warm coat of the alpha, her nose nestled into his side. His torn ear twitched as he slumbered.

The goddess watched. For the first time, she did not spare a glance for the strange fruit dangling so tantalizingly above her grasp. If it had dropped to the earth, she may not have even heard it land.

Still, that night she did not sleep for the longing.

⌒

The girl's name was Impatien. She was fully grown but still in the blossoms of youth.

On a night when the white fruit had shriveled to half its size, the goddess waited until the wolves were asleep and awoke Impatien. She took her by the hand and led her to a sunken pool of clear water not far from the den.

During the day it was green because of the soft plants that coated the rocks, but at night everything was colorless. From mossy banks overhead, water fell in elegant columns, and dark alcoves of privacy hid tucked behind them.

The goddess and Impatien stopped at the edge, for the girl realized she could not go into the water with her clothing on. She gazed desperately at the midnight pool until the goddess helped her undress.

The goddess's hands trembled. Impatien's wide eyes glistened in the dim light, but she did not stop the goddess.

The goddess rested one arm across the girl's bare back and stooped to place the other behind her knees, lifting her. She studied Impatien's full lips as she carried her.

By the time the water reached her hips, they were kissing.

When Impatien's body dipped beneath the surface, the goddess released her knees to work one hand through the girl's sweet-smelling hair. Impatien was hesitant and shy, but she did not stop the goddess.

It was only when the goddess began walking them toward the waterfall and the dark recess behind it that they looked up and saw the eyes.

Two yellow eyes glinted from the trees. Then another pair, and another.

The wolves had followed.

Before the goddess could stop her, Impatien slipped between her arms, dove beneath the water, and swam back to the land. She grasped her clothes and bounded into the woods.

⌒

The girl stayed farther from the goddess after that. It only made the goddess want her more.

One night Impatien lay in the pile of wolves, her breath fogging slightly between her rosy lips. She slept fitfully, her pale skin flushed and blooming.

When the goddess looked to the sky, the fruit was nowhere to be seen. The place it usually hung ached with hollowness. She looked at the girl, then back at the empty sky. With every desire that was ever in her, the goddess longed for a taste.

She closed her eyes, pursed her lips, and sang through her throat. Her howl cleaved the night and spread it wide.

⌒

When the white fruit had seeded and begun to blossom once again, the goddess could no longer wait.

That evening she fed her wolves the berries of a sleeping tree, and when the strange white fruit hung farthest from reach, they all snored softly outside the den. It was then that she woke Impatien and led her to the pool.

This time the girl took off her own clothes, and the goddess stepped with her into the startling embrace of water. They walked along the fuzzy rocks until they reached the waterfall. Impatien was hesitant to cross beneath the noisy fall, but the goddess coaxed her.

There, hidden in shadows, the goddess finally tasted.

⌒

The wolves did not awake until the next night. The goddess was out hunting in the woods when she heard Impatien's cry. It stopped abruptly, followed by the snapping sound of bones and snarls. Silence hung like a spoiled fruit clinging impossibly to its branch, and then the wolves began to howl.

⌒

The goddess knew she could no longer lie down among the wolves. She tread softly through the forest. Instead of loping into view of the pack, she climbed up over the back of their den and sat. They would scent her eventually and she would have to choose, but for now she was content to look down upon them where they piled in sleep, muzzles slick with red.

She yearned to thread her hands through their soft, shaggy manes and let them warm her cold skin once again. Instead, she looked up to the sky, where the strange fruit hung ripening.

Beneath her, the wolves awoke and began to howl. Their throaty voices called, begged, seduced the untasted flesh that gleamed white and mysterious.

The goddess lifted one hand, but her fingertips touched emptiness.

It was not enough.

THE GODDESS OF BIRDS AND WIND

by Alex Shvartsman

You seek not the goddess, but the proof that she doesn't exist.

Your detractors brand you as an atheist and a malcontent. Your few supporters smirk knowingly and prattle about the difficulties of proving a negative. The indifferent majority thinks you a fool for your efforts.

You are not deterred.

The concept of a higher power, the idea that something exists that is grander than a human spirit offends you. There is no goddess: there are only tall tales from the ancients shivering by the fire, and the migratory patterns of birds.

You struggle to fund an expedition to the far ends of the wilderness, where the goddess is said to reside. You seethe at the ignorant who refer to your cause as the "mission to find the goddess," but you hold your tongue as you can ill-afford to antagonize the few willing to make donations.

Once you set off on your journey, you travel for weeks, far away from the cities and towns, make your way on horseback beyond the smallest rural settlements, walk the uncharted paths until even the local guides will go no farther. They speak in their gruff dialect and point at the gray sky, and their eyes widen in fear. You leave them behind and press on.

When you reach the thousand-year-old forest spoken of in legends, you make camp and you wait. You push back doubt, for what evidence can you gather of a deity that isn't real? But you persist; returning with your head held high, having survived a fortnight in this place, will have meaning. Over time, opinions will change, believers will be swayed. For only after it casts its superstitions aside, can humanity rise as high as the gods it once imagined.

And then you suddenly know, with absolute certainty, that you were wrong.

You feel the presence of the goddess before she arrives. There is a change in the air that heralds her advent: the sky darkens and the breeze chills, and everything is sharper and somehow more real. There is a stirring in your soul, a longing in your loins, and your skin tingles as though it's being traversed by an army of ants.

You want to act—to run, to hide, to scream at the top of your lungs—but you can't. You stand there and you wait, letting the gusts of icy air slap your face as you crane your neck and stare up into the heavens.

Then you see them—a pair of black dots zigzagging against the gray background of the clouds. Their flight pattern is erratic and ragged, and as they get closer, you can make out the details: their feathers, and talons, and beaks. Their wings beat fast against the elements and your heart thumps as it tries to match their frantic pace. From your vantage point, you can't quite see their eyes, and of that you're glad.

They're only the first. You hear the rest before you can see them, a cacophony of caws and beating wings that builds up from a whisper into a crescendo as a black mass appears on the horizon, and grows steadily, inevitably, until it blots out the sky. Thousands of birds are hurtling past you, not so much flying as being swept up by the gale, dragged along by the will and purpose of the goddess.

Your senses are overwhelmed, your emotions conflicted. There's fear and fascination and the primal urge to drop to your knees and worship her, but the most powerful emotion—the one that takes root in your heart, builds up in your chest, and swells up until it dominates your very being—is anger.

You stand straighter, defiantly facing the storm, and you rage against it. You are human. You are different. You are precious. Your sentience separates you from the frenzied flocks above. You make your own choices rather than be carried along by the whims of some higher power. You shout these things until your throat is hoarse and raw, but the wind beats against your face, stealing your words and carrying them off like so many unfortunate crows.

Then you glimpse the goddess herself for the first time, and you cease shouting. Your mind, your intelligence, the very thing that makes you unique and special, fails utterly. The goddess is an idea personified, a being of more than three dimensions, a presence that is vast and overbearing. Your mind's attempt to interpret what your eyes are seeing is like trying to pour a river into a cup.

There is a taste of salt and copper in your mouth. You realize that you bit deep into your inner lip, and blood is seeping down your throat. But the goddess is getting closer now, and you ignore the taste and the pain. Her presence fills the world around you, pushing away fear and comprehension and reason until there is no room for anything but her.

She overwhelms you completely. You buckle to your knees, and then prostrate yourself on the ground, face pressed into a pile of damp leaves, your hands clawing at the earth, grime collecting under your fingernails.

You no longer struggle. Instead, you let her power wash over you like the high tide at full moon. You embrace the savagery and the inevitability of it, until you revel in it. You begin to laugh, decaying oak leaves brushing up against your teeth.

Time passes. Moments? Eons? You don't care. The windrow of rotting leaves embraces you like a down comforter. Then the goddess's presence subsides like the morning tide, and pain rushes in to fill the void.

You prop yourself up, scraping the soft underside of your forearms against the twigs and debris, and you watch the flocks of birds being carried away from you by the storm.

At first, there is a twinge of relief. But it doesn't last—it's drowned out by sorrow, and longing, and profound loss. The goddess has moved on but, having communed with her once, you will forever miss her. You feel as though the most important part of yourself has been ripped away, leaving you forlorn and brittle in the wind.

You scramble to your feet and you chase after her, prodded on by the squalls. You shed your clothes and your skin and your very being as you run. You flap your arms wildly, until black feathers protrude from your flesh and your nose hardens and twists, and your bones become light and hollow, and your body collapses into itself until only a small avian form is left. And then you take flight, your wings spread wide against the howling currents of algid air. You leave behind solid ground and mortal concerns, and you soar ever higher toward the clouds, pursuing the goddess.

And then there is only her, the birds, and the wind.

GODS OF EMPTY PLACES

by A. T. Greenblatt

Jamie was the first of us to give a piece of herself to the gods of empty places. She started by trimming the tip of her left ring finger. She assured us it was painless, though my brother and I saw her winced when the knife touched skin. I couldn't help but wonder if it had pained our mother too when she use to give up slivers of herself.

Our mother. She wouldn't have approved of Jamie's sacrifice, but our paper boat was sinking. The water pooled around our feet. We didn't know what else to do. So, we held our breath as we leaned against the ship's banisters and watched that tiny part of Jamie slip into the endless ocean.

At first, I wasn't sure if it worked, if Jamie had given enough. But slowly, the puddles around our feet stopped growing, then started to recede, and our vulnerable ship stayed afloat.

My sister, my brother, and I exhaled and thanked our hollow gods, making sure to leave long pauses between our words. We gazed across the inky ocean, straining our eyes for any sign of land.

As usual, we found none.

So we sailed on.

☊

I had wanted to cross the ocean for a long time.

Our first raft was made from the usual things; wood, cloth, rope. But when we lowered it from the pier, the dark water swallowed it whole. Next, we tried metal, carefully curved, tested, and researched. It sunk faster than the raft.

In frustration, we built a boat from my journals, Ben's drawings, and Jamie's favorite books. Our hopes and aspirations lay bare in plain sight, but I didn't care. By that point, our mother had finally sacrificed too much and without her, there was no reason to stay on her tiny, overpopulated island. Now that she was gone, I thought I had nothing more to lose.

I expected the worst when we lowered the paper boat into the water. But the gods of empty places are ironic and merciful when they choose to be.

Back then, I didn't think to ask why.

Instead, I laughed as we set sail, brimming with newfound freedom. Our mother had traveled across the ocean to search for a new, untouched home, and now her children were finally doing the same.

⌒

The next time the boat sprung a leak, I made the sacrifice to the gods, stepping in front of my brother Ben. Taking the knife from his hand. Determined to always be the rebellious little sister first. I gave the gods of empty places the nib of my nose. It came off easily, bloodlessly, like it wanted to go. But instead of dropping it into the ocean like Jamie, I used that little piece of me to stop the leak in the hull. It held.

Ben watched me, not quite hiding his worried expression. "The look suits you, Lana," he said.

"Jealous?" I teased. He didn't answer, but his eyes studied my face, that place where I wasn't anymore.

The next time water started seeping in, he trimmed his pinkie toe without hesitation and threw it up into the sky. My brother, the artist, always loved the empty places above.

⌒

The paper of our boat was already full of ink, but I wrote in the spaces in between anyway. I kept careful records of the weather, the ocean's moods, and our conversations. Of the three of us, I was the rebel and the memory keeper. The boat, naturally, was my idea.

But on the quiet days, the empty days, sometimes I wrote to our mother. We never agreed, my mother and I, but still I missed her.

For years, we'd watched her grow thinner as more and more lost people washed up on her island. I know she'd hoped we would stay there after she faded away. I did try, really, I did. But there was something waiting for me beyond the dark water.

So now, I wrote to my mother where I could. All the questions I should have thought to ask her before she faded away.

⌢

Our boat kept leaking. So, bit by bit, my brother, sister, and I relinquished ourselves to the gods of empty places. Jamie gave herself to the water, Ben to the sky, and me to our boat. We skimmed and cropped and snipped without complaint. In the long afternoons, we laughed and admired how the sunlight shimmied through the gaps between where we were and weren't.

Only our brother sometimes seemed sad after a sacrifice, though he never said why. He refused to cut his right hand, his drawing hand, though he gave the gods the rest of himself freely. Jamie and I teased him for it, but we understood too. I kept just enough of my fingers to hold paper and write.

Together we held back the leaks and sailed on in our impossible ship, eagerly waiting for our boat to scrape against a new and empty shore. And I'd smile because I thought I understood the gods and their empty places.

I didn't understand a thing.

⌢

Our mother taught us that there were gods for everything; a god for flowers budding in the shade, a god for walking safely with untied shoes. She told us we weren't like the others and that everything we wanted in this life we'd have to make ourselves. She warned us that the gods of empty places were the most benevolent and the most fearsome.

I didn't learn to fear them until we had lost too much. Not until my siblings and I had become diminutive, mostly holes and voids.

And the leaks kept coming. Still, there was no land in sight.

⌢

Jamie was the first to go. She was no more than a sliver, a shadow now.

"Don't leave us," I pleaded.

"I won't," she promised. A curl of a smile formed on what was left of her lips. Before I could stop her, she slipped into the ceaseless water and disappeared.

Our ship didn't leak for many days after that. Ben and I didn't speak much, didn't laugh anymore. Though our sister was thin, the empty space she left behind was too large for words.

⌒

Ben left next. He disappeared in the middle of the night like a traitor and a thief, except he was neither of those things. I knew he hadn't sunk into the water like Jamie. "Don't fade away just yet, little sister," he'd scrawled on the mast. I think he knew all along that he would never see land again.

In one of the few blank spaces left on our boat, I wrote to my mother: *How did you make it across?*

She didn't answer. Neither did her gods. But the sky was clear and calm for many nights afterwards.

⌒

I took me a long time to understand empty places. How to find land.

Our mother never wanted us to cross the ocean, but she taught us about the gods all the same. Taught us how to make things. To give freely. Our mother taught us this because she knew her children were too much like her.

Eventually, the emptiness, the loneliness became unbearable. So one day, I tore down my boat, page by page. I laid them flat on the water, edges overlapping slightly. The island I made was tiny, but it grew as I methodically dismantled my boat. The paper didn't sink and I didn't sink when I walked across it. I wasn't surprised; the gods of empty places must have understood what I meant to do, because in the morning the island was no longer made of ink-filled paper and dreams, but of rich earth and fresh water.

I used it all for the island, except for three pages, one for each of us. From them, I shaped children, as my mother must have done so long ago. They are small, fragile things now, but they will grow.

They are already walking, asking questions, their paper bodies already becoming flesh. They already gaze longingly at the ocean.

I am thin and know I will become thinner still. Soon, others will start washing up on this shore, desperate for a home, and I won't refuse them because now I understand what it's like to be lost at sea. And one day, when I finally fade away, I doubt my children will stay on this new shore.

But I thank our hollow gods anyway because my sister, brother, and I have finally found our home in the vast space between the ocean and the sky. I thank them because I know that whatever my children choose, one day they'll find their place, their purpose in the emptiness too.

THE BOY WHO DROWNED

by Duke Kimball

The People give presents to The Boy Who Drowned and wait to see if he will kill them.

He stands on the shore of The Lake, antlers pale with moonlight. Tall, tree bark skin and mouthless. The People are waiting with treasures laid out on hides of elk and deer; he can feel their trembling breaths as he slowly surveys the offerings. Every year, he comes. Some years he accepts their gifts and recedes back into the waters. Other years, his displeasure is visited on them in carnage and blood.

"Ghost Rabbit," the Elder calls him this, the name of some new god. They do not know his name. He doesn't remember it himself. "We beg, be kind to us! We bring you our very best!"

The Boy Who Drowned groans in fury. He cares not for their best. They flinch from him, uncomprehending. He understands them, they do not understand him. They never understand. They never bring him what he wants.

There are bad years, lean years, when The People bring him food, and skins, and even their own young. Boring things, rotting things. Nothing to soothe him from the hate, the hate, the hate. Nothing to keep his medicine from violence.

This year is good. Bone knives, many bone knives, polished stone axe heads and spears. Shiny things, lasting things. And then among the good things, nearly lost in a tuft of elk hair, The Boy spies the best thing.

Small yet precious, a single bead of ancient black glass, almost perfectly round. The Boy Who Drowned bends down to take a closer look

and the black bead is the center of his mother's eye. Her hand holding him firmly under the waters, his chest burning, then sputtering to the surface just when he is ready to slide into unconsciousness. "The longer you hold your breath, child, the more powerful your medicine becomes." His father, watching his seventh son from the shore with disapproval. Not daring to say anything against her. His mother's medicine is strong. The Boy's is not. Not yet.

He wants this. The Boy Who Drowned takes the bead gingerly in long, inhuman fingers

and he is below the waves, alone, again, forever, always, to prove to his mother he can grow stronger. The world tunneling into dark, the fire in his lungs fading to dull ache, the world moving closer until it is one black point, now gripped in his palm.

They never give him what he wants. But this—this will do for now. He walks back into The Lake. The People behind him give prayers of thanks and pack up their hides. Safe, again, for now.

Safe, it is safe beneath The Lake. He hardly needs to breathe now, he waits hours, then days, then months before stealing ragged gasps from the surface. He waits for a hand to push him down, eyes filled with medicine and fire, but they don't come. Where have they gone? His medicine grows and so does he, taking the flesh and wood and bone from hapless rotting things, making them better, stronger, lasting. Part of his self. His mother will be proud of his medicine, his mother will be proud, his mother...

The Boy Who Drowned dives further on and in and on, the black bead dulling the hate, the cold. Still he longs, still he needs. He is not strong enough. He cannot be. Not yet.

With each passing year, passing breath, he searches for her, but finds only strangers. Weak, tiny things. Filled with fear and empty words. They try and placate him with cheap, tawdry presents. He wants to kill them, hates them, needs to kill them, needs.

Where is my mother?

He keens in the depths.

Why have they taken my mother from me?

In his palm, in his chest, his medicine burns, and he holds in his breath for one more year.

SEEN AND NOT HEARD

by Barbara A. Barnett

She is just a statue, I tell myself, though I swear I can feel hot blood pulsing beneath her surface. The Goddess Vasdahr: Eater of Worlds, c. 3050 BC, artist unknown. Clay sculpture. 6 x 2 x 2 inches.

For years, the statue languished in a forgotten corner of the museum, in an unmarked crate full of heavy black dirt. It was only through the time and tear of age that the wood cracked, the dirt poured forth, and Vasdahr made herself known to me.

She is a tiny thing, unusually detailed for the period. At first glance, she looks to be no more than a woman of her time and place: tall and dark and slender, her sheath dress adorned with feathers and beads, hair hidden beneath a tightly wrapped head cloth, mouth curved in an inviting smile. But on closer inspection, I notice the other mouths—one on the palm of each hand, gaping maws lined with fangs. A shiver runs through me when I touch them.

"She is just a statue," I say, and set to work—the one thing I refused to let Mother cow me out of pursuing.

⌒

"Playing in the dirt with those boys," Mother said that Easter morning when my cousins and I decided to dig for dinosaur bones in the backyard. She straightened the pink sash around my waist and refastened my barrettes until they yanked at my roots, hard enough to make my head throb. "You're lucky you didn't ruin your dress."

Mother grabbed my hands. I tried to pull them away, but Mother held them tight as always, fingers digging into flesh. She scowled at the grime caked beneath my nails.

"You know what this means, don't you?"

I could only nod.

"No dinner for you again," she said as she locked me in the hall closet. "Seen and not heard, young lady. That's all you need to be."

⌒

It is the power of suggestion, I am sure, that makes my stomach rumble as I work, cleaning away too many years of dirt, careful not to chip the paint beneath. I scrub at a stubborn patch on the statue's right hand. Right mouth? Is there a difference for Vasdahr?

Mouth and hand, I think, looking at my own hands, so plain and powerless in comparison. *Voice and action. Command and consume.*

The dirt is unyielding, and so I scrub harder. The clay breaks, and I cry out.

"No, no, no...."

My voice trails off as thick red liquid, dark as night, pools around the fracture. Blood? It can't be, I think, touching a finger to it. Cold, yet a feeling like fire shoots through me. Desire and hunger for all that Vasdahr has to offer. A way to be heard.

I put the statue to my lips and drink the blood of a goddess.

⌒

I tried to be heard on their terms.

I just wanted to make a suggestion about the Kamau Collection, I wrote to the museum director one morning. Mother's voice haunted me as I typed. I was being too bold, getting above myself. It was unbecoming. Unattractive. No wonder I was still alone. *There are unmarked crates we might consider doing an inventory of. I think it's very possible we'll find artifacts of value.*

The director's response was quick: "We don't have the time or the manpower."

Then, at the next staff meeting, one of my colleagues loosened his tie and said we should inventory the rest of the Kamau Collection instead of letting it rot away in storage. There was bound to be something of value in those crates.

The director's response was quick: "Good thinking. Draw up a plan and get on that."

"But I already did." My voice was soft, cringingly close to meek, yet they stared at me as if I was screaming. "In the proposal I sent. I had a timeline, and a workflow, and—"

"Whoa, nobody's stealing your ideas, Dee. We're all on the same team here."

Yet they continued as if I had never spoken at all.

Seen and not heard, Mother, aren't you ever so proud?

⌒

An itching begins in my palms, painful at first, then arousing. Something moves beneath my skin.

"Yes," I say, and let the statue fall to the floor and shatter.

I scratch at my palms, harder and harder until the flesh tears away and the teeth push through. The skin in the middle blackens and flakes away. At last, I stare down into the gullets of my new mouths, overwhelmed with hunger.

With only a touch of my hands, I begin to eat—my tools, my chair, the table, even the shards of the goddess I have become. They all taste of blood and honey. I shudder with pleasure, and yet it is not enough.

"More," I whisper with my new mouths. "I want so much more."

Beyond this room, I hear voices trying to drown out my own. I devour the walls with my hands and step into their world.

This woman was just a statue, I will tell them. And then I will learn what it is to command, to consume, and to have my voice heard through all three of my mouths.

TIPS FOR HOW TO DEAL WITH YOUR DAUGHTER WHEN SHE'S BECOME A MONSTER

by Gwendolyn Kiste

Do your best not to scream when you find her in the basement rec room with the three neighbor boys.

Or with what's left of the boys anyhow.

☹

"I didn't mean to," Livia whispers.

The radiator hums along the baseboard, and you don't speak. Neither does your husband or Livia or the trio of stone statues that once passed for high school seniors. Track stars, football stars, stars in the hearts of all the swoony schoolgirls.

Stars to nobody now.

You lean against the doorway to steady yourself. One too many gin-and-tonics buzz in your head. Tonight was an evening out for you and your husband, a rare moment for just the two of you. You almost never leave your daughter alone. You don't know what she'll get into. You certainly didn't suspect it would be this.

Livia shivers and fidgets barefoot on the cold tile and wipes a clot of tear-soaked hair from her eyes.

"I never touched them," she says. "All I did was look at them."

But that's not all they did. Her shirt is torn in the front, and there are fingernail marks across her chest.

You can guess the rest.

Livia sniffles. "I'm okay, Mom," she says, even though you didn't ask.

His face red, your husband hollers at the statues and pounds his fists on them, as though they only need a little coercing to return to life. When that doesn't work, he paces wild circles about the room, mumbling incoherently at Livia.

But you can't afford to be incoherent. You're her mother. You have to know what to do.

So you take your daughter's hand, and lead her upstairs to the bathroom where you dab iodine on her cuts. Your heart in your throat, you don't ask questions. And you don't look directly at her. You're afraid of what you'll see.

"They said all they wanted was to watch movies with me," Livia murmurs. "And I believed them."

You nod and say nothing. This is ridiculous, and you know it. You should scream or sob or do something, *anything*. But you don't. Staying quiet seems like the safest option.

As you put away the bottle of iodine, your hands shaking, you catch a glimpse of Livia in the bathroom mirror. Her hair is wild, her face sallow. She's only fifteen, but she looks so much older tonight. You wonder if she'll always look older now.

"Come on," you say, the first words you've spoken to her this evening.

You tuck your daughter into bed before returning to the basement. Your husband is still there, trying to reason with the stone boys or with God or with anyone else who might listen.

"What has she done?" he asks, but you only shake your head. You tell yourself to stay calm. Besides, what else can you do? You can't help the boys now, and you can't call their parents or the police. They'll take Livia away from you. They'll blame her for this.

You try not to blame her too. Your little girl who's forever doing strange things. Singing a lullaby that makes your ears bleed when she's happy. Shattering a mirror without touching it when she's sad. Always with an obscure look drifting behind her eyes.

Perhaps tonight is just the latest stage in metamorphosis for someone like Livia.

"What happens now?" your husband whispers.

"To them?" you ask. "Or to her?"

⌒

Don't panic. It might seem advisable at this stage, but please refrain.

⌒

In the morning, you pretend everything is normal. You don't ground Livia for what she's done. You simply don't talk about it.

After your husband kisses you goodbye, you retreat to the kitchen and drop an apple in Livia's bag.

"Don't forget your lunch," you call after her.

This feels like your entire life: reminding her who she is and what's expected of her.

Without you, everything would fall apart.

She swipes her bag from the counter and slams the front door behind her. You close your eyes and hold your breath and try not to think anything cruel about your daughter.

You fail.

She shouldn't have been alone with them. She should have known better. How did you raise such a foolish child, one who's always making messes?

The stone boys are still in the basement. Hidden away, they've already become your filthy secret, like a cache of old VHS pornos.

You slip downstairs and examine their faces.

This one had a football scholarship in the fall to Purdue.

That one was a soloist in the church choir.

The other volunteered at the soup kitchen on weekends, always smiling, always saying the right things.

Ask anybody in the neighborhood: these were nice boys, normal boys. But you wouldn't ask, because you knew the truth. They'd grown up in the backyards you could see through your kitchen window. These were boys with wandering hands, good for pushing and pinching and other things—worse things—now that they were older and stronger.

But thanks to Livia, they won't get any older. They'll stay eighteen forever. She flashed them a poisonous glare, and that was enough.

Your breath catches. How many dirty looks has she given you over the years? Too many to count, probably.

"Your face will stick that way," you used to tell her, and you were half right. Her face didn't stick. But theirs did.

The sun dips in the sky, and your husband returns from work to find you still staring at the boys in the basement.

"What do you think they're made of now?" you ask.

He shrugs. "Does it matter?"

"I guess not," you say, but you wonder if that's true.

⌢

Keep quiet. Whatever you do, never say the truth.

⌢

You wanted more children, a whole houseful of them. To stain your carpet with grape juice and to smudge their greasy hands across freshly cleaned windows.

But you only got Livia. A child with moonlight in her blood and dirges in her heart.

"Why can't she just be like other girls?" you'd ask yourself in the mirror when you thought she couldn't hear you.

For dinner tonight, you decide to cook a roast. A roast will fix everything. Before Livia gets home, you drive to the grocery store. On the way inside, you pass one of the boys' mothers. Her mascara streaked down to her chin, she's stapling up *Missing* signs to the community bulletin board. She stops to tell you it's probably all a prank the boys are pulling, and you think how *prank* is a funny word for what they did.

She talks to you a long time, what might as well be an eternity, and when she's done, you flash her a pinched smile and tell her you'll keep her family in your thoughts. You don't say all the things you want to. Not *it's already too late* or *I hope you hurt like I hurt* or *how dare you raise a son like him.*

Instead, you pick out your pork loin and stand in line and think how you don't have long now. You have to figure out how to hide this.

Back home, with the roast in the oven, you return once again to the basement.

"What do we do with them?" you ask. They're too big, too cumbersome to transport easily.

"We'll hire someone," your husband says. "Movers from out of state. They won't suspect they're anything other than normal statues."

But nothing about the boys looks normal anymore. They're more grotesque than you remember, with the claw-like curve of their fingers, and the way their lips twist into grimaces. Were they afraid of Livia for even a moment, or did they never suspect what was coming?

After dinner, you collapse on the upstairs couch, desperate for a moment alone. You don't get it. Livia creeps into the room and curls up in your lap. Without thinking, you run your fingers through her hair.

"Don't worry," she says.

"About what?" you ask, not looking at her.

"I'd never hurt you." Her voice is thin and faraway. "I didn't even want to hurt them."

⌢

Don't get angry with her. Don't blame her. Remember: she's still your little girl.

⌢

There is no rhythm to your days now. Only the useless commands to a daughter who refuses to listen.

Pick up your room, Livia.

Pack your own lunch, Livia

Don't disappoint us and convict us and ruin everything, Livia.

Don't be who you are, Livia.

The police are going door to door now. They'll get to your house soon. Maybe tonight, maybe tomorrow. They'll find them here. They'll find the truth.

You turn off all the lights and sneak to the basement. Livia is already there.

"You don't belong down here," you say, your gaze steady on the wall behind her.

"Where do I belong?" she asks without inflection.

"Nowhere," you say before you can stop yourself.

But it's true. She would belong with you, if she'd ever done what you asked. But she didn't, and now you don't even recognize this stranger. This monster in your midst.

You grit your teeth, and for an instant, you wish your daughter out of existence.

"This is your fault," you say. "You did this to us."

Everything in the room goes still. Livia turns and stares into you, and you look at her for what feels like the first time.

"Yes, I did this," she says, her eyes dark, and there isn't a hint of regret in her voice. Of course, there isn't. She didn't start this. They did. She only finished it.

Something tightens deep within you. *You.* The one who failed. The one who couldn't protect her. Who didn't even try.

You never asked if she was okay.

You never asked how it happened.

You never asked anything at all. You wouldn't even look at her. You worried more about the boys—what they'd done and what to do with them—than about Livia.

All the fury inside you dissolves at once, and your cheeks burn with shame. You want to rewind your life. You want to do better. Most of all, you want to beg your daughter's forgiveness.

But you don't have to. Livia asks nothing from you, except what you already are: her mother. She doesn't need anything else. She already knows how to fix this mess. Without a word, she places one hand on the nearest boy's shoulder and shoves.

His stone body topples to the floor and shatters into a thousand pieces. Then she moves on to the next and to the one after that, until they're all reduced to rubble.

"There," she says, and smiles. "All better."

⌢

Take them to the ocean or the lake or even a wide river. Bring a picnic lunch perhaps, and make a day of it.

⌢

As a family, you give the boys to the water. You pack them up in garbage bags and duffel bags and bright pink beach bags, and when no one's looking, you drive to the shore and toss them bit by bit into the waves.

Her sandals kicked off in the sand, Livia takes the flattest pieces— fragments of eyeballs and toenails and Adam's apples—and skips them across the water.

"Did you see how far he went, Mom?" she asks, giggling. "Almost to the moon!"

You shield your face from the sun and smile at her. Even if pieces of the boys resurface, no one will recognize them now. And this far from home, no one would ever suspect Livia.

Your husband stands with you, his arms looped around your waist. He doesn't ask what comes next. Neither do you.

All the two of you know is that this is your little girl, dancing and chortling on the shore.

You can't protect her. You can't save her from herself.

But with that dark look still waiting, still drifting, behind her eyes, maybe you don't have to worry.

AN ILLUSION OF SUBSTANCE

by C.M. Muller

As we left Cinéma Les Nemours, I could still sense Anne-Marie's dismay as to my having cut short our inaugural evening stroll through Annecy to take in a French thriller called *La Gorgone*. The irony, of course, was that I missed the majority of the film, the old theater's plush seating accommodating my jet lag a bit too well. I was still groggy as we re-emerged into a now night-eclipsed Annecy, lit up and busier than ever. A crowd of onlookers filled the main square, their attention rapt on what appeared to be a public statue. They were surrounding it completely, as though to prevent its escape, and for the life of me I couldn't understand the intrigue. I looked to Anne-Marie and could tell by her expression that she knew perfectly well what was going on. She took me by the arm, leading me closer, ignoring my inquiries. As I said, the crowd was spellbound, especially the few children who were out at this late hour. From what I could tell, it was nothing more than the patinated figure of a man who, judging by his clothes and hat, might very well have been some important individual from Annecy's past, even though I saw no plaque distinguishing him as such. What struck me as strange was that I did not remember seeing the exhibit when we had first passed through the square. My initial thought was that it was a dedication ceremony of sorts, that by some incredible means the monument had been heaved into place as I slept through *La Gorgone*. Anne-Marie and I stepped as close as the crowd would allow, and it was only when the figure's head shifted slightly downward, its right hand angling toward a bowl of coins, that I fully understood what was happening. The crowd, acting as a single entity, produced the expected laudatory cry of awe, thereafter dropping coins into the bowl. I sensed Anne-Marie staring at me, and could tell that she had been doing so for the entirety of the act. As we turned from the scene and began making our way toward the hotel, she explained in greater detail the oddity I had just witnessed, stating the importance of the living statue, that it was a serious and time-honored vocation in Europe and beyond, artists going to great lengths to cast themselves in long-term immobile roles, not only in the paints they selected to cover their bodies, but in the manner in which they developed their muscles and breathing to approximate stillness, to give an illusion of substance. I grew more and more fascinated by the topic, and later, as we lay in bed watching French television, I could not shake my admiration for such a profession. When I shifted closer to Anne-Marie, with the hope of attending to her own statuesque beauty, I found that she had already fallen asleep. I returned to my side of the bed, flipping through channels for nearly an hour before finally turning off the set. At first, the darkness seemed as impenetrable as stone, and no matter how hard I tried I could not divert my thoughts from the idea of a living statue. At some point, having grown irritated by the persistent ghostly presence, I felt that I had no choice but to rise from bed and wander about our inordinately quiet room—and then, in a moment of surprising spontaneity, out the front door and into the town itself. Even though I could sense the cool evening air upon my skin, I knew that I had to be dreaming, because it truly felt as though I were floating over the cobbled lanes, a skeletal kite being drawn by hidden string into the very heart of Annecy, into the now crowdless space of the living statue. He, or rather *it*, stared at me for the longest time, sizing me up without once moving its eyes, the intensity of its focus strengthening with each beat of my heart. I remained as still as stone, waiting for movement, cowering like a child beneath a father's unapproving gaze. Then the eyes suddenly clamped shut, their black lids seeming to expand like twin boils of ink intent on nothing more than the complete obliteration of all my senses.

When I finally regained consciousness it was to an overwhelming brightness followed by the startled expressions of a group of onlookers, young and old, encircling me. I tried to move, but the only limb which felt mobile at this stage was my left arm. It was pointing at the empty bowl on the ground before me. The audience, largely unimpressed, began to disperse and the bowl remained coinless. I tried to close my eyes, though found this an impossible task. Growing increasingly aware of time, particularly its slow passage, I desperately wished to crack from this shell and enjoy the freedom that had once been mine. More than anything, however, I longed for Anne-Marie, desired to glimpse her gentle eyes, sure that her presence would awaken me from this nightmare. As it happened, I didn't have to wait long. She stepped into my field of vision, close enough to peer into my eyes. I tried to speak, and the longing, the *need*, to do just that must have been clearly evident somewhere in my blank expression, for I could detect a look of quiet horror in her features, a flash of terrible understanding. Or was it relief? I attempted unsuccessfully to shift my arms in order to embrace her, to comfort what I assumed was a growing trepidation. But all her worry disappeared with the arrival of a man who set himself far too closely to her side, arm wrapped snugly about her waist. Such intimate contact made her smile, and as the interloper turned to have a better look at me, I realized the full horror of the matter, for I had glimpsed just such a countenance thousands of times in any number of mirrors. The sheer terror of being unable to close my eyes at that moment was impossible to bear, and the scream that so desperately sought release was encased completely, unutterably, in the stony musculature of my new skin.

IRIS AND CHIAROSCURO

by Erin Robinson

Lady Cecilia Sebold swept past the parlor clerk into the studio while I was practicing washes inspired by sunlight shifting through a green-glass bottle half full of olives.

Without a glance to my mistress, the renowned miniaturist, Ms. Vera Webster, Lady Sebold claimed the central dais and posed one pearl-white finger by her temple. The better to admire the *beaux-arts* gracing the walls. *Adoration of Beauty*, some might paint her, until they noticed the stock she surveyed: browning sketches and half-finished portraits. Yet she flicked the sapphire drop in her ear and glided to one—my attempt at a young woman startled from prayers after last Sunday's service, her rapture blunted.

A column had hidden what disturbed her. Rather than venture forward, I'd fumbled for the charcoal nib I always tucked amongst my hatband ribbons. I'd forgotten I'd no paper left save pages from Vera's treatise, *An Artist's Plea Against the Acceptance of Shadows as Art*. It was her stand against that new alchemy, the daguerreotype, and zealots who bent all to capture the sun. They aimed to arrest its light and harden it darker than burnt egg on a plate. I'd marked my copy almost beyond reading and wouldn't tear the blank corner preserved for one final flash of thought. Even one that flickered as I dashed home from church. So I ripped a poster for *Douglas & Blackburn's* from the brickwork of *Sprague's Stationery* and scrawled upon its backside.

Now Lady Sebold considered the maze out of which I'd re-made that woman's face. Each curve braided a dozen stray lines. The most wayward freckle I'd refused to smudge out. For every stroke unspooled another until the whole wove together. If you stepped back.

Lady Sebold pressed closer. Her breath quivered the paper's unpinned edges. And I sloshed my wash water onto the table.

We both reached, me for a cloth to sop up my spill and she for a charcoal curl that may have been a loose ringlet fallen across the maiden's cheek. Or a smile's fading arch. No matter. Lady Sebold smothered my line with her finger and followed it to the full lips.

My breath stopped.

I braved a glance at my mistress. Her brush shook Mars-Red drops down her palette, but she noticed my look and turned away.

Lady Sebold had read Vera's treatise. She admired her work. Praised her skill at coloring life. Truth, she once said, was in the tints. I dared not reproach her if Vera sat mute. But when that unflinching lady blanched at the black smear on her finger, I breathed again. A short inhalation before she chose the maiden's other cheek and blushed it with the char from her finger.

Wet seeped over my palm. Hurriedly, I wrung the cloth over the washbowl as Lady Sebold wrung a hoarse word from Vera. Then she whirled. Her sea-green skirts swished my easel's legs as she billowed away, and I bowed my head—*bowed*—and tugged my apron over off-white patches in my gray skirt.

"Vanity," Vera muttered, and her brush seemed to writhe in her hand.

For another quarter hour, we painted. Our brushes plunked and clattered against palettes and mixing trays. At the clock's chime, Vera stilled. With her back to me, she cleaned her brush and made her excuse. Another round of calls to wealthy tradesmen and their wives. Another attempt to woo them to our art.

If she returned, it would be late, so I could paint on or lock up as it pleased me. She'd know my progress by my strokes, though I had trouble gauging hers. Three months had passed since the last new patron sat for us, yet Vera had bought two portable cases with actual drawers for scrapers, pencils, even a folding ruler, as well as two washbowls, forty paint blocks, and slots for nineteen of those new color tubes. Some clients preferred that we paint them in their homes, as Vera must be, but the visits wilted her. More than once she'd borrowed a short spear from our props to straighten her hobble.

I used to accompany her. Now she insisted I was better used in the studio in case someone called. Hers was the established name, but one day soon mine would rival it. She'd promised me.

I tried to focus on the olive bottle. Strange that its green should have so few shades of olive in it. Forest, myrtle, asparagus, cheese mold—

My study slurred. Lines, crosshatched, seethed into serpents. Unable to separate heads from tails, I scrubbed them away then found myself staring at the *Startled Maiden*'s clouded cheek.

Once we might have broken with Lady Sebold for her desecration, even of my modest sketch. But ever since the daguerreotypists raised altars to golden Sol and his light, the blind had flocked into their shadows, lured by pledges of silvered life. They never saw the copper plate beneath the sheen. And if, by chance, they glimpsed a metallic glint about the eyes, they mistook it for evidence of soul.

That evening, I prayed for sunset's blaze, and the gods sent me a vermilion fire striated with Indian and chrome yellows, and a flush of rose-pink in the exact hue Vera had feathered on the cherub-cheeked portraits of Lady Sebold's daughters.

In a month, she'd bring us her toddling son, and she wouldn't need to hide beneath a sheet and squeeze him so he couldn't move while a cold lens fixed his semblance. No, he would crawl and coo into his likeness and remember the burbling joy of his infant self long after liver spots inked his skin.

That was our power. Our pact with the gods—that we would glean the essence of their gifts to this child, that woman, and not fetter someone to a moment, but slip him through the span between one breath and the next. Offer him the animate whole of life when so many favored a suspension.

That night the gods whispered through my dreams. I woke with sunrise flaming through the slats, and heat pulsing limbs I couldn't still. I dressed but let my hair slither in its braid, certain that I'd fumble pins and cut myself. Certain I would bleed quicksilver.

In the studio, tremors plagued my hands, and I had to hold my breath and stipple between heartbeats. I tried a broad chrome-yellow wash, but the gods scratched with the bristles, *Cloud the eye, Petra Vitale. Black it to jet.*

Overdone olives festered as I waited for Vera to take her leave. They rotted entirely afterward and were a ball in the bin before the hour. At the chime, I drew my chosen brush from the water.

It glistened. Wider than the others, its breadth firmed my arm. I sheathed it and a tube of Lantern Black in the largest of Vera's prop reticules then stuffed my braid beneath the broadest hat brim on the stand. Thus outfitted, I turned to the *Startled Maiden.*

Had the gods upset her prayers to answer mine? I did not pause to doubt but lifted the lower corner and read the address for *Douglas & Blackburn's.*

Anywhere in the city, the softest mention of that den conjured crowds. I'd never lingered. What did I care where daguerreotypists laired? I'd no means to strike at them. Except my art.

Outside, my skirts flapped around my heels, but I hesitated a shop away. Gawkers, transfixed by the sight inside a window, guarded the path.

I clutched my reticule and, eyes averted, stepped around them.

No one barred the next door, but inside, immobile faces marbled soaring walls. A gallery of daguerreotypes framed in gold, which outshone the palette of lead and ash.

I headed for a second door. As I passed each face, it colored, reflecting my hat's emerald green, my skin's pale peach. Until a seated child usurped my peach with a rose-pink of the exact hue that feathered the Sebold girls' cherub cheeks.

I froze before the tinted image.

When a girl bustled in, smelling of ammonia—and burnt coffee, it seemed, but that couldn't be right—I cracked my fingers from the reticule's strap.

"Oh no, miss," she said. "Accounts are settled after. Once you're satisfied."

I reproduced her smile, and she blinked—"Just so"—then led me into a receiving room where two young men ogled the painted women on the walls.

Here then was the pinnacle of alchemy: women petrified to perfection then reanimated by vibrant strokes. No common hand had accomplished this.

I wavered, and the girl helped me to a chair. She asked if I'd been troubled by that charlatan next door. "A sorry show, miss, his *Phantasmagoria*—moving slides, very poorly painted—those magic lanterns, gorgons to our goddess. You know the tale, miss? Never mind. There's no telling those as mass to him. Would Miss consider frames until her time? These gentlemen's friend is nearly finished."

I shook my head, no, and she left through a third door.

Within the hour, a man entered, carrying an engraved case and the winking squint of someone forced to look upon the sun. His friends shielded him, but I heard my summons from the chamber.

Rising, I tugged the hat brim low over my eyes and tucked back snaking ringlets. I crept past the door into a shaft of light—a moment of exposure—then a terrible screeching began.

I shied to the wall. Above me, three women rent the air. I recognized the mirror first, angled from the wall, then the girl reflected in it, and two women with several ropes connected to more hanging mirrors and sheets of blue glass. The women adjusted them to redirect sunbeams from a skylight and dilute their rays. Pulleys shrilled.

I exhaled but continued to edge around the room, hunting my quarry in mirrors. Halfway around, I saw it, perched on a tripod. A dark habit veiled the cursed head but not that monstrous eye.

I opened my reticule and drew out the brush. *Now*, the gods hissed. *With the sisters distracted.*

I untwisted the tube cap, plunged my brush against the surge of black—

A wash-stained hand clamped my arm. Every blotch and vein of it had been painted as often as my own. Hard fingers squeezed, and I looked into Vera's graying eyes.

My brush slipped from my fist.

Vera caught it and led me to a couch, where a woman—Phoebe Blackburn—warned me to rest my hands upon my lap lest the stirrings of my lungs cloud my skin's subtle shadows.

The girl—Phaedra Douglas—smiled as she fitted my neck to an iron collar on a stand. "Better to hold you still, miss."

I could have fled, but Phaedra tilted my chin—"Just so"—and Phoebe angled the camera, and Vera, who'd shown me how three colors woke infinite worlds, made a note about my flaxen hair then took her foreshortened place at their feet.

Against this triptych, I drew a breath—coffee and ammonia and heat. For the length of a sitting, I could be stone. Afterwards, I'd fracture enough leg to wing home before my face shattered, and gods alone knew what emerged.

WE DID ALL WE COULD FOR THEM

by Rebecca Ann Jordan

WE

When our husbands are monsters, we sit on the porches for long afternoons, enjoying the quiet fullness of our company. This looks like: knitting, avoiding knitting, aimless gossip, teaching each other how to make little objects we can hold in our hands when we are missing our husbands before sleep.

All except Edina. When her husband is monstrous, Edina goes down our one red road to the sheds, coming up to the suburbs three times a day to make meals. She spends the rest of her hours beside her monster's shed, hand-feeding him through the bars. A few of us went down when he was particularly hairy.

"Edina," we said. "Come away from there. We have cool lemonade."

She sat on a stool, dressed fully to her wrists and ankles in solitary yellow, though the day was hot. "Thank you, my friends." Edina was much too pale to be out in the sun.

"Right now he isn't in his right mind," we reasoned, trying not to look directly into his eyes that were pits. This time he looked mainly himself, a bit thicker-haired as he paced. He opened his mouth; we caught a glimpse of rows and rows of fangs within. His tongue was all cut up on it from trying to speak. His mouth closed and leaked blood.

In a shed nearby, another monster honked and wheezed and howled.

Edina folded her hands in her lap, and sweat, and sweat some more. "But he will be soon. He is still my same Nathaniel." Red road dust made her lips mountainous.

Edina's husband came to sit on the ledge of his cage, legs alternating bars. We dared not hear his moans. "Think of your daughter," we implored. "What will she learn from your sitting here, indulging him in his monstrous time?"

"My daughter," Edina said, eyes closed against the bright sun, "will see that I protect the innocent in their most difficult times."

We gave up then and went back up to our homes, arm-in-arm, shaking our heads in pity for Edina. Some people did not want to be helped. Her marriage was young, but her life would be agonizingly long if she wasted it down by the sheds every time her husband changed.

⌒

LEISEL

Not long after my father shed the last of his monstrosity and returned home, my mother became sick. My father called in a city doctor, wringing his hands all the while, but the city doctor gave us a bottle of pills and told us to make her chew them and swallow. I didn't trust what change might come on her if we did, for good or for worse, even though my father begged me to let him feed them to her. The doctor had a way of licking his lips that made me unsure if he was monstrous and someone had forgot to cage him.

We compromised and called the country doctors. They pulled me aside as my father stood over my mother's bed, praying to his god of science.

"Leisel," they told me, "wasn't it true your mother went down to the sheds during your father's changing-time?"

I nodded, remembering those long nights alone, when the walls of the house seemed to shift and my mother wasn't there to hold them up. "She always does. She protects him when he's in his madness."

The country doctors shook their heads. "Leisel," they told me, "you must not let your mother go down again. She's touched the man in his madness, and his demons have danced on her skin."

After they left, I went upstairs and watched the hunched back of my father bent over the bed, stroking back my mother's pale hair. Her breath fluttered like a bird with a broken wing. She smiled at my father's touch, coughed. We had opened the windows so she would feel the sun's touch, and shafts of light cut her diagonally, lighting on her eyelashes.

I stepped inside and my father turned around. "Um," I said, and told him what I thought should be done.

He raised his hand, but passed without ruffling my hair, and I only felt the lapping wave of his perfumed air as he left to lock himself away.

⌒

EDINA

In my sickness I dreamed of him. He: body-warm, and you'd think what I'd remember most is his shark-rows of teeth. But in the dream we were in a house made of glass, and I walked about it, naked. I asked him if he wanted to sleep with me. Maybe later, he said. He smelled of splinters so I held my breath. A massive train was coming, and he kept trying to tug me by the hand away from the window, toward the center of the house and a fortress of mattresses. But I wanted to see its coming. To press my flesh against the glass and feel its rattling back and forth, the threat of breaking. I wanted the worst to happen. It to shatter inside of me. The only sound was the hiss of my husband behind me, begging for my comfort. I knew without looking he had grown to a size almost as big as the house, and he wanted to hide me behind his arms thick as pillows, his blanket-spine and bedframe hips, his vaulted ribs and the soft creaking of his toes. I woke before the train could pass by the windows, to my daughter leaning over me, touching my feverish forehead. I asked for him. Where was he? Throat full of mucus, barely able to speak.

⌒

TERESA

In the night I let the monsters out. One by one my hand went through their fur. They only responded to my touch, mine, their howling snouts rooting about for my scent. My blood theirs to taste. Their horns mine for the taking.

Tonight there was a new monster snuffling like a pig for acorns in the corner of his cage. "Come on." I coaxed him with a bit of red cake. It was my birthday and I wanted to celebrate.

He lingered, larval eyes like dark jewels. But when I opened his cage he knew I meant him no harm.

He dragged himself out with stumpy legs like an anteater's. "That's it," I murmured. I let his seeking tongue find me, curled like a question. A honk from his mouth that sounded like "Mama."

It wasn't as if any spoke of it afterward, especially not new monsters with brains incompletely formed. Afterward, when they were out of their monster time and put on their human skins like slipping into suits, we'd pass by each other on the dirt road and he'd not let out a peep. Just bounce his glance off my hands, perfectly manicured. And who could tell if it was the very same whose body I'd delighted in the night before? They were hardly ever recognizable.

I'll admit perhaps there was some memory of coupling, a certain ache in his groin where before there was none, a flash of teeth under moonlight. But you never heard him complain.

⌒

MADGE

I woke and a beast dripped slime onto my chest. Next the smell: oil, salt—unwashed. In the flesh of his first change, my son crouched above me, a mass of scales, smooth but sickened, gleaming green-and-white striped by the yellow light from the bathroom. He lifted a long snout—no mouth, no teeth, no claws. Nose to my chin, trembling: a low blurt.

He couldn't be blamed—it was his first change, and he was so young. Twelve gentle winters. "Hubert," I said, low to pacify him. There was no way of knowing what sort of monster he might be. Gentle? Violent? Hungry? Jealous? "Get down. To the floor."

Hubert's black eyes were emotionless, rimmed by his scales—smooth as a pangolin.

"Go on."

He backed up and I relaxed. What was it the other women had told me to do? I had taken a class in preparation for rearing a son, but all its knowledge seemed to flee now, leaving my brain empty and prone to instinct. He stood there, all fours, hunch-backed, slavering on the latch-hook rug: twining, thorny roses. A ropy tail sloped behind him like a dead limb.

I wiped the drool from my chest, onto my pajama bottoms. And tried not to think of the disease the monsters carried, of the demons that danced on their every surface and Edina sick abed. Even worse, I worried about the hardwood floors—newly installed—but his paws were scaly stumps, smooth but clawless, ineffectual.

Keeping my voice low: "Hubert, it's your time. You have to go to the sheds."

His long snout, tapir-like, coiled and rose, curved up. A horrible howling sound.

On these rare occasions I longed for a husband.

I should have been better prepared, but all I had nearby was a broom with a long, angled handle. This I grabbed and thrust the end toward my son. He did not fear me; why should he? He didn't even flinch; the handle struck his side. The howling stopped and he scrambled back. "Go on, Hubert. Go on."

Some run to the sheds, some must be dragged. My son, I drove him outside, for the first time but not the last. He tripped down the steps onto the midnight road. So rare, I've heard, for men to change at night, preferring the heat of the sun for transformation. He honked at me, lowered his body to scrape his belly along the road. I bruised him. But it was for his own good, though he was too stupid in this body to understand. I drove him on, and on I drove him to the sheds, howling all the way.

⌒

WE

As the sun set, we sat on the porch, reading quietly, some of us watching viral videos and withholding giggles so as to not disturb the others, some of us doing budgets or working on our freelance jobs, those of us who worked from home for businesses in the city. It was a balmy early evening, that kind of pad-footed friendliness that came with an impending weekend. The men were inside, playing their frivolous games—wrestling, philosophizing, betting, waging theoretical wars.

Edina was recovering from her illness, rocking in a chair and listening with eyes closed to our chatter. Laurel pressed her forehead to Teresa's, murmuring of plans—broken plans of the past, plans to be broken in the future. Madge decorated Leisel's ankles with tattoos—she cried and giggled. We were drunk enough to hallucinate a few things, imagining we could see the rising, gleaming city from here, imagining we could taste its tastes and smell its smells. But we did not hallucinate the monster that tiptoed past our porch.

"Hey," we called to it. It was a mass of dark fur, so that we couldn't see eyes or nose or mouth or even arms. Two legs bunched beneath this mass, and above, two coiling horns like polished wood. It crouched, halting its journey to turn its horns to us.

We were in a kind mood, unafraid of consequences due to the wine changing our blood to courage. We didn't know whose husband he was. Mabel wanted to pet it. Leisel wanted to know if it had a tongue. Teresa wanted to test its horns.

But it looked frightened, and so we called out to it: "Come, monster-husband. We won't harm you. Come up to the porch; we have wine."

The trembling thing's hairs rose, puffed up around it like a hairy sun. Then it turned and ran on its two man's legs, hard down the road to the sheds.

We thought, *that is what we get for treating a monster with respect.* So we never invited our monsters to our porches again.

ONLY THE MIRRORS TELL YOU

by Rhonda Eikamp

Much later he took Route 90 south, as the dark site had suggested, and thirty miles past La Bogue, turned off at the derelict Texaco station. The emptiness ate into wetland, bald cypresses hunching above him swathed in their moss scarves like grieving grandmothers. The Puma rattled on the pockmarked road. It was a brain tumor of a car, a thirty-five-year-old man's bad shot at rebellion. Maybe he'd sell it when he got back. The thought made him tremble. He could go back. Call the police.

They wouldn't see it. Not without mirrors.

Like dusk, the swamp arrived too fast. The house, when he found it, was more than a shack, not quite a house. A drunken porch ran the length of it, knee-walking into the boggy water that stagnated at the southern end. Paint peeled from the clapboard walls in gelatinous strips, as though the swamp periodically swallowed the house to the roof and spit it back up.

To both sides of the porch steps, on makeshift clotheslines, hung what Sam prayed were thick black ropes.

The man who clambered from the porch rocker as he approached was short and lanky, with a filthy blond beard. Somehow Sam had expected large, larger than himself. The guy was younger than him too, not much over twenty. A kid.

And the black ropes of course were long, long snakes. Water moccasins, he was pretty sure. Ten or twelve. Decapitated, hanging stiff with their own weight. Dead, you know they're dead. Black capillaries, varicose veins stripped from the ageless swamp body and hung to drain.

He wouldn't lose it now, couldn't, not after everything.

As he stepped between the poles, staring, unable not to stare, one headless snake bled a single drop into the crabgrass.

"I make belts out of dem." The kid held out his hand. "Name's Henry."

He hesitated. He'd used a fake name on the site, but then he remembered: truth. "Sam."

"Well, Sam."

Sam spoke the word that had been on the site. The grays in Henry's eyes changed. Welcoming, admiring. "I am mighty proud to hear it, Sam. Wanna come in?"

Go in, ask him the special questions he mentioned, leave. Just until the tremble in his veins stopped.

The inside of the house was even wetter, not in moisture but decrepitude, a geriatric drool of neglect. A table, tiny kitchenette, sofa like a compost heap, grayed to match its owner's eyes. A door to a back room stood open a crack, darkness falling out, bogging Sam's mind.

"I should call you brudder."

Not that. He was nobody's brother. Wouldn't be. "You were the first one, weren't you?" Sam surprised himself with his question, with the gummy taste in his mouth. With getting straight to the point.

"I was first to learn how to see dem right." The accent made Sam think the kid had said rot. "Dey're very canaille, sneaky, but you know dat. Wanna beer?" From a top-notch fridge entirely out of place amid the gunk Henry produced two cans. When he turned back, his gaze landed on Sam's hands, clamping hard on a chair back, and an air of fungal wisdom coalesced about him. Henry was older than he'd guessed, Sam realized. "Sit down, friend. You should take a breath, celebrate."

They were in fact a family, if you believed the voice on the site. In fact and in soul. The smallest of families. If you believed. Eleven others had found their way to the site. Sam lurked for over a year, reading comments, the experiences, telling himself he wasn't. Taken. Turned. This will resonate with you. If you are. His mother barged in once and he'd clicked away too fast. What's that? Nothing. Well, come down to supper. It hadn't stopped her asking again. And again. And screaming. And the tears. One of their worst arguments. Not the worst. If you loved me, you wouldn't have secrets, she'd wailed.

"You been crazy brave, my friend. You gotta believe it. Couyon, de world would say—just crazy. But we know."

"It's just.... You said there were things a person would need to know. Afterwards." The word stuck in his dry throat. "Things you'd only explain in person." Persons, brothers, strangers to one another but for the acknowledgement, the deed. And Sam was one now, and wasn't, and the trembling wouldn't stop. "I just...."

Henry's grimace was sly. "Show you sometin."

The freezer side of the fridge, when Henry opened it, was black with bulging cancers. Thick dark rings stacked atop one another. He extracted one and placed it before Sam. A coiled frozen snake. The ice snake's scrape against the table belied its tumescence, its obscene organic sheen. Dead, you know it's dead. The beer in Sam's mouth was sludge. You were a prisoner, hypnotized. That's how it worked.

"Keeps 'em fresh till I find time for skinning. Just too many."

Hypnotized by the back room, a few feet from him over there. Mesmerized by the gnaw of the wrongness and rightness, the writhing in his gut.

Henry saw his glance. "Come on. Time to take a look."

Time to see. The back room Henry threw open was clean, like a different household. A green banker's lamp warped the shadows. A long table in the middle, with something long on it. There had been no photos on the site, the nameless moderator—Henry—claiming no one but true family would see anyway. Approaching, Sam felt his legs battling an ocean current, the bog again. It was deep need that had hypnotized him so many years, paralyzed him. She'd always been beautiful and ugly. Good and bad, sacrificing when he was young, forever night shifts at the hospital, then needing the sweets afterwards, and a mother deserved something didn't she, a child would think that. And later, when she couldn't work. He'd tried in his twenties, tried so hard. Women, who eventually always realized, their eyes changing, as Henry's had but in the opposite direction, jerking toward dismay, even if they didn't grasp the extent of it. She was sick for awhile, see. Couldn't live alone. I stayed on. The reasons weren't reasons. The women would make excuses, not call back.

Henry's dead mother lay face-up on the table, nude. No trace of the blood the large damascened hunting knife buried in her chest would have called forth. Behind Sam, Henry was mumbling the secret truths from the site, the abductions at birth, false sons held captive all their lives, draped in illusion. Unable to see it. No trace of rot in the corpse, Sam realized, though she would have been the first to go, two—three—years ago, after Henry made the discovery and created his site. The dead woman was bald, as though shaven, black spots the size of quarters covering her scalp. Only in mirrors, Henry catechized behind him, in the right light would a man see. The woman's death rictus, contorting the skin all the way to the crow's-feet around her glassy open eyes, rendered her face hideous.

Sam's mother had always cut his hair. She sat him in a chair in the bathroom. He said, I should start going to a barber, and she had turned, half-finished, and touched his shoulder the way she did. The mirror had showed him then what he knew: a blur sliding by, reeds of broken light, red tongue slivers darting. The ugliness. When you see, act fast before you turn to stone. The shears lay by the sink where she'd left them and he spun and stabbed with his eyes closed, finding the neck. It fought him. Its strength was shocking. The heavy braids slithered against his arm, viscid, alive in their true nature, and hissed. When he opened his eyes at last to stillness, the face was hers again. Dead, you know she's dead.

As Sam watched, the black spots on the bald woman's scalp pulsed and he realized they were holes, taut skins of new snakes congealing and pushing as they sought to free their heads. Sea creatures not quite breaching, the brain a seething serpentine mass. One broke through as he stared, the head slapping against the scalp as it peered about, tongue darting. Whole worlds of nausea burst inside him. He no longer knew how he came to be where he was, when all the things that someone else had twisted up inside him became too tangled for him to ever unknot.

"Cut 'em away all you want, damn snakes keep on coming."

Henry stood close behind him, his voice gentle, familial.

"Why you cain't just bury her. Dey'll come right out of de ground."

He imagined the bathroom floor she lay on a writhing nest by now, filling up.

"You gotta go back, take care of it, keep killing dem snakes."

But Sam didn't move, he was turning to stone and had been all his life, watching snakes spurt and detach, filling the bathroom and then the world, for the rest of his life nothing but snakes forever.

BLUEBEARD'S SURRENDER

by Julie C. Day

There are over 2900 species of snakes in this world. The rough-scaled bush viper is one of the twenty-five percent-ers, poisonous from the moment it's born. And though it's true that ability doesn't infer intent any more than predilection equates with action, the muttered you-can do-it of such creatures always seethes below the surface. Perrault's Bluebeard made the same bloody choice with each of his seven wives. In the end the secrets behind locked doors are always revealed.

So it should come as no surprise that Aisling Marillier's bedroom housed a reptile—a bearded dragon—by the time she was eight, even though Aisling's mother, Temperance, had been very clear. Temperance had no interest in thawed mice carcasses or the needs of pinky-mice-famished snakes. But Aisling, with Bluebird-like tenacity, pressed on.

"Snakes don't even have eyelids, Mommy. They never close their eyes. Isn't that cool?"

"Sure, baby. I guess. But not in this house."

What Temperance liked best was *The Real Housewives of Beverly Hills* and a not-so-secret Salem menthol after Aisling went to bed. But eventually Aisling's bearded dragon was also okay. Unlike all those pet-store snakes, Dragon Echidna liked to wave hello. At least that was Temperance's take after one too many Aisling-soliloquies concerning the ventral scales and flexible jaws of Aisling's close-held passion.

Aisling actually liked Dragon Echidna. And for whatever dumb reason, she really tried to make it work. But a lizard's scales don't differentiate into shields and plates. Its tongue remains unforked, and always it refuses to slither.

Best friends, as it turned out, didn't help at all. Even when they'd known you for fifteen goddamn years.

"Chad, I've had Echidna since I was in second grade. Dude, that's seven years of explaining that Echidna's wave is a submission stance." Aisling sat on her twin bed, legs stretched out, trying to keep them still. "She's unbelievable. Mom actually thinks Echidna is her friend. Ball pythons are much more social. Plus I'm old enough to handle the mice thing myself." Aisling glanced at Chad and frowned. Instead of looking at her, he was riffling through her topmost desk drawer.

"Chad?"

"Yeah?" He glanced at Aisling, an almost blank stare, and then returned to the desk, pulling out a yellow-and-brown beetle encased in resin, followed by an old friendship bracelet, and finally the petal-covered stationery box Aisling had had since she was five.

"Look can you just focus for a second on what I'm fucking saying? Ball pythons are shy. They definitely won't squeeze you to death. They don't even grow that big. I'm more than old enough."

"I don't know, Aisling. I think your mom's got a point. Reptiles aren't like dogs. They don't give a shit about us." Chad lifted the lid off the old stationery box and stared in seeming disbelief. "Really? Still with the snakeskins?"

"Chad, stop trying to change the subject. You know I did the research on ball pythons!"

"Thing is, I'm just not sure you did it all that well," he replied in his most reasonable tone.

"Jesus. I really don't know why I put up with you." Aisling felt a strange ache in her jaw, a sense that her hair and skin no longer belonged on her maturing skull. But Aisling's problem wasn't aching bones or pawed-over tchotchkes. Aisling's biggest problem was Chad himself. He wouldn't stop inserting his bullshit ideas into her life.

In the end, a bearded dragon, not matter how badass, can only scratch a girl's viperous itch for so long.

"Echidna's dead?! Chad, why didn't you text me? I told you the motel had cell service." Aisling stood in the apartment's open doorway, feeling a cool spring breeze wrap itself around her neck and shoulders. Had she cracked her bedroom window before she'd left?

"I'm sorry. I don't even know how the heat lamp got knocked out of place. It's not like I killed the thing on purpose."

But Chad looked uncomfortable rather than sorry. And he hadn't even bothered to use Echidna's name.

Aisling's mom stepped between them. "Here, dear, take the cash. You did what you could." She handed Chad his pet-sitting cash. And then Chad was out the door, heading home with his twenty dollars and her mother's thanks in his ears.

"He must feel awful. The least I can do is pay him," Temperance said, as though disappointed in Aisling for being upset.

Dead stays dead, a sibilant voice whispered as Aisling stared at Echidna's empty cage. *You can't ever take dead back.*

Now that was a viewpoint that made some sense. Dead definitely stayed dead every time.

The blue-gray haze appeared that very night, the one Chad and Temperance didn't seem to notice even when Aisling was near. The one that seemed to require sunglasses for longer periods of time each day. And then the school year was over, done, gone, along with teachers, and bus drivers, and afterschool friends.

Down by the river, while Temperance was at work, it was just Aisling, the water snakes, and, of course, her oldest friend, the ever-present Chad.

⌒

The wetlands that ran alongside the Farsdale River was filled with smooth-barked maples and birches. The cries of wrens and warblers interwove with the steady thrum of cicadas hiding in the long grasses.

Water snakes lounged in curving masses on the thin stretch of mud flats that flanked the Farsdale riverbank. Patterned snakelets not much bigger than a shoestring sprawled among the darker bodies of the adults. When Chad and Aisling were sick of each other's voices—or when Chad was sick of his own—Aisling would count the increasing number of snakes while Chad skimmed rocks through the river's shallows.

"Fifty-seven on the ground," Aisling reported. "Five more than yesterday." She adjusted her sunglasses and raised her face to the sun's midday heat.

"Where the hell do they come from? Look at them. They're a fucking hazard." Chad scowled as he picked up a nearby stick.

"This is their spot as much as yours," Aisling replied, not really meaning it.

"They're pests," Chad insisted, poking at one of the smaller snakes. He took a sudden step back as it hissed, mouth wide open, fangs revealed.

"Right." Aisling adjusted her sunglasses, walked to the water's edge, and grabbed a nearby maple's lowest branch.

"Aisling, what are you doing?"

"Haven't finished the count. Snakes love trees." She moved her lips upward, pretending a smile, then hoisted herself into the maple's crook. Farther out from the trunk, water snakes rested in the branches that overhung the river.

"Fuckers are gonna get you."

"They're completely non-venomous," Aisling said. The skin around her skull felt tight, her mouth overly full. "Vicious bite though..." Was that a lisp?

"Your shirt's all smeared with tree crap," Chad opted. "White was a stupid choice." He wandered toward the river and onto the nearby dock.

"I guess." Aisling removed her sunglasses and looked down at Chad. It felt so damn good. Aisling's sclera—the whites—had vanished four days ago. Her eyelids, the bruised-red of drying rose petals, had dropped off two days later. Now Aisling's vision was protected by a milky ocular scale. Now she was certain. The haze would completely clear after her final shed. Aisling the Scaled. Aisling the Reptilian Viper.

"Hard to tell the difference between water snakes and the more poisonous fuckers," Chad warned as Aisling inched over the water along one of the thickest of the maple branches and its tangle of serpents.

"Does it matter?" Aisling tried to subdue the lingering S sound for just a bit longer.

"I guess not...if you're an idiot." Chad sounded bored, almost sleepy, but Aisling and her lidless eyes weren't fooled. He was watching for her response, sure he knew what it would be.

"Ha ha, funny man." Aisling smiled, her lips held carefully together.

"Just trying to be helpful."

Stretched out over the slow-moving river, the maple's bark felt as smooth as a snakelet's scales. Aisling knew her snake lore. It took some time for a hatchling's roughness to appear. It took time for their skin-nub of an egg tooth to drop from their mouths so they could speak unfettered. That was the reason her transformation had taken so long. She'd needed that time to form the necessary hardness.

Up in her maple tree, Aisling felt the sun-warmed scales of a water snake slide across her legs while another, untroubled, watched her from only inches away.

Snakes, Aisling knew, tasted heat. They saw best at night, when teenage girls and their secret dreams blossomed forth. And on days like today, when the snakes were writhing, Aisling couldn't think of anything quite so beautiful. Those night-girl voices deserved to be heard. Forget Chad and his oh-so-helpful comments, she had a few of her own.

When Aisling lunged, it wasn't a game or a dare. It was an explosion of movement, followed by a thrashing in the shallows before the arms, his arms—finally—sank below, and Aisling joined all those girls with their slitted nostrils and eyes that lacked the merest hint of white prowling the riverbank and its trees.

Bye-bye, baby boy. Bye-bye, my not-so-true friend. Snakes knew how to care for themselves from the first minutes of birth. They didn't back down and they definitely didn't show any mercy. True snake fact: they didn't even attempt to listen or understand.

BURNING BRIGHT

by Carina Bissett

There are two identical doors. Behind one is a lady. Behind the other is a tiger.

Which door will you choose? The one on the right, or the one on the left?

Eeny, meeny, miny, mo.

⌒

A stray gust of wind needled through an eyelet in the tent, which fueled the flame just enough that it was able to reach up to scrape its teeth across her belly, severing the thread that held her skin in place. She fell in a heap of fur and bones to the arena floor. The crowd fell silent for a moment and then roared to life as her trainer snapped the fierce black whip near her face.

"Vega, Vega!" The man's voice was all iron bars and prodding forks. "Up, Vega!"

She shifted to a kneeling position, but kept her stomach close to the floor. Her ears flattened against her skull and her lips peeled back in a snarl. The tyger trainer stepped forward and snapped the whip, closer this time. She knew the drill. The trainer might go easy on her if she succumbed now, so she staggered to her feet. Perhaps this was how she'd escape, Vega thought as she waited for her insides to slip through the seams.

Nothing happened.

A flicker of amusement flashed across the tyger tamer's face before his gaze hardened. He forced her through the rest of the routine, an act that revolved around her—Vega, his rising Star.

The crowd cheered.

⌒

Sometimes a girl is born in a skin that doesn't fit quite right. It might be too loose or too tight. Bias cut missing; a hem sewn too short. When this happens, when a girl is born in an ill-fitting skin, she has a choice. She can force herself to endure what she cannot disguise. Or, she can tear it apart at the seams, cut a new shape to fit a pattern of her own choosing.

Sometimes a girl is born in a skin that doesn't fit quite right, but she never gets the chance to make a choice.

Someone else makes it for her.

⌒

The girl froze in place, but it was too late. A line of red looped around her wrist, a noose pulled tight in a trap she hadn't seen. Her free hand hovered in the air, fingers curled to catch a Star woven from a simple string. The noose tightened.

"You belong to me now," said the boy.

His voice was light whereas his touch was not.

The girl's heart fluttered, but still she didn't move. With her palm facing down, her pulse remained hidden. For now.

"Say it," he said. "Say you're mine."

That scarlet string pressed harder, so hard that her bones ached.

It had started simply enough. Cradle. Rabbit. Diamond. Crown.

Keeping the line taunt, the boy slipped a knot to close the loop. He checked the tension and then added a whole line of knots, one after the other, like beads on a string.

Hunter. Candle. Dragon. Flame.

She searched back through the blur of figures, but she still couldn't see it, that moment when a simple child's game had turned into something else.

The boy brought her hand to his mouth. "Mine," he whispered, the syllable igniting like sulphur sparked to flame. Languidly, he pulled the string between his teeth and severed the loop, leaving the girl at the end of a leash. "You belong to me now."

The boy turned her palm over. He kissed the tender skin with lips firm as the flesh of a plum. The noose slipped beneath her skin and threaded into her veins. The boy measured out a length of red as the knotted skein followed the radial pathway to the girl's heart. The boy tugged on the string and, once he was certain that it was firmly anchored, he swallowed the other end.

"Say it," he said.

The girl drew in a thin, reedy breath.

The boy raked his teeth along her breastbone. His tongue followed, branding her with a trail of leisurely kisses. His eyes were closed. Contentment rumbled deep in his chest.

Tiger. That was the figure he'd camouflaged with clever fingers. No. Not Tiger, but Tyger. A seductive assault. A proclamation of love. Dizzy with the revelation, the girl exhaled and gave him what he wanted.

⌒

The merry-go-round spins and spins. The mirrors reflect a menagerie of fabulous beasts painted with decorative colors that startle the imagination. How vivid! How bold!

The horses with their jeweled harnesses and cotton-candy colors are accompanied by giraffes, deer, ostriches, dragons, and tigers. Something as beautiful as a hand-carved unicorn must be guarded from vandals, protected from the elements. The poles speared through the creatures keep them steady; the bolts pinning hoof and claw to the floor are an added safety measure.

The lights! The mirrors! A dizzying spectacle of color and charm. The merry-go-round just keeps spinning, one revolution after another. And at the center, the calliope screams.

⌒

Back in the tight confines of her cage, Vega began to groom herself. Her search for the thread led to the discovery of scarlet stitches that zippered her from tongue to tail. They had not been there before.

The trainer and his newest assistant paused near the beast wagon. The iron bars mocked her own stripes, but failed to hide her from prying eyes.

"Is she okay?" The assistant carried buckets filled with the scent of old blood.

"She's young." The trainer tapped a long metal fork against the bars. "It won't happen again."

Even though the threat ruffled her fur, Vega concentrated on unravelling the red thread that held her together.

"Vega will do as I command."

Metal rapped against metal as the trainer sought to capture the tyger's attention. "She belongs to me. She has always belonged to me."

At that, Vega paused with the sudden realization that she'd understood every word, every single one. Hidden beneath the black-and orange-striped fur, the shadow of another life stretched, reaching for freedom. Vega held the thread between sharp teeth and pulled.

⌢

Even though linings seem like a luxury, any decent dressmaker will tell you that a proper lining is an important step in the sewing process, one that you shouldn't skip. This silky layer is attached to the outer garment and serves many functions: hiding raw edges and internal seams, providing a slippery surface that makes it easier to dress and undress, and keeping areas of tension such as the knees and seat from sagging or stretching.

Although most linings are "invisible," that doesn't mean you shouldn't have some fun with them. Some people choose a lining fabric that matches the garment, but there's no reason you can't select a contrasting color or print instead. Go wild. You'll be glad you did.

⌢

"I love you," the boy said in between kisses that rained down like blows.

He had found her hiding under the pelt of the tiger he'd killed on safari. Hunched over beneath the weight of that orange- and black-striped fur, the girl had spent the afternoon picking at a loose thread she'd found under the bruises that mottled her breasts. She'd pulled and pulled; a pool of red string unraveling in her lap. But no matter how hard she'd yanked on that slender strand, the knots around her heart held.

The boy ripped the pelt from her shoulders and his passion exploded, scoring her in a blaze of white heat. He wrapped his hands around her wrists and forced her to her knees.

"I will never let you go." The boy looped the thread around her, wrapping it tightly around her breasts, her hips, her thighs. "Never."

Under the pressure of his kisses, the bindings sank beneath her skin. The boy caressed the new bruises left behind.

Outside the open window, the stars wept silver streaks against the backdrop of the night sky. The scent of jasmine crept into the room to comfort the girl, but even those sweet notes couldn't mask the mingled odors of sex and blood clinging to her skin.

"You belong to me," the boy said when he finished. "You will always belong to me."

⌒

Girls go missing all the time.
Some of them return.
Some of them return more than once.

⌒

During the next performance, the tyger shone brighter than any Star.

"Vega, Vega!" The whip cracked.

The tyger jumped higher, ran faster.

Why do you make me do this? A fist bruised. A spark ignited. The memory burned. A girl held up outstretched fingers, skin tinted orange in the late afternoon light. Get up. Another blow fell. The world shattered.

"Up Vega!"

The tyger roared, setting black stripes rattling against her bony frame. She leaped.

The timing was perfect.

As Vega passed through the blazing ring, she shed the tyger skin and landed right on cue, only this time on two feet instead of four.

Out in the grandstands, beyond the glare of the circus lights, the red wet mouth of anticipation swallowed the audience whole. The trainer's eyes widened. The whip fell from his fingers.

Vega snatched it from the sawdust and easily balanced the heavy handle in her human hand. She grinned, teeth bared, as the whip sliced through the air between them.

The thread snapped.

THE WALLFLOWERS

by Lora Gray

When you open your eyes, the daisies are watching you.

They droop beside the hospital window in the chipped blue vase that normally resides on the kitchen counter between the plastic surgery pamphlets and Meg's ceramic roosters. An artificial breeze stirs their petals and you share a slow nod of solidarity even though you are green and new and they are beginning to wilt.

When was the last time anyone watered them? When was the last time Meg visited you? Two days? Three? You try to picture her, to remember the angle of her eyes or the way her mouth curls at the corners when she's upset, like she's tugging the emotion back down her throat, but you can't. Her face is as blurry as an unfocused photograph. Maybe it's because of the morphine drip. Maybe it's the chlorophyll. Or maybe it's because Meg keeps changing and you just can't puzzle her together in your head anymore.

Meg abandoned the natural curve of her cheek on her thirty-fifth birthday. She sucked away the soft pillow of her tummy as a gift to herself too. Then it was the lavender eyes. Then the stiletto implants, her newly spiked feet punching dents in the bedroom floor. Last month she got Medusa Extensions. You've been bitten a dozen times by her hair.

Who knows what else she's had done since you last saw her. Will you even recognize her when she finally returns?

If she returns. She hadn't really wanted you to do this, after all.

The hospital gown crinkles as you carefully unfurl the leaves that were once your hands. You've traded bone for plant fiber the way Meg traded hair for snakes and the long stalk beneath your hospital gown seems at once frighteningly foreign and gloriously flexible. The doctors say it will take some getting used to, but there are places for you to heal and adjust after you are discharged. Therapy gardens to take root in. Transitional arboretums. Rehabilitation hothouses and carefully tended conservatories with mindfulness coaches. Green places. Quiet places with fields full of people just like you to silence the noise of never belonging.

You've yearned for quietness for so long. You shrank into classroom corners as a child. You faded into dorm doorways at university. You barricaded yourself behind potted ferns at your first office job. You tried to hide behind the decorations at your wedding reception, terrified that one of the glittering fashionistas Meg worked with or the endless parade of power couples joined, literally, at the hip, would notice you and sneer. *How boring,* they'd think. *How plain. How passé.*

Meg smoothed her hands over your face and sighed as if you were a precious, hopeless tragedy. "Let me dye your hair at least," she said. "You'll be so much happier without all that gray. You'll see. Everybody will notice."

But you didn't want to be noticed.

After thirteen years of marriage, Meg still doesn't understand that. Even when she finally, grudgingly, accepted the reality of your first and only surgery, she said, "But why a daisy? They're just so cheap. Why not a lily? Oh! Or an orchid! Something exotic. Something really beautiful."

Meg's powder room is a paper garden of beautiful people and tips on how to become them, their photos and magazine articles clipped and taped to every wall and mirror. *Cheekbones That Wow! Be a REAL Tigress in the Bedroom! This Year's Top 10 Sexiest Plastic Surgeries-Hydro Hips and Diamond Fingertips!* Every surface is overgrown with images of lilac eyes and rose bud breasts. Noses carefully sculpted into Eifel Towers. Chins carved into the pyramids at Giza. Swatches of synthetic skin in every conceivable shade, fresh colors screaming to be seen and loved.

On the hospital windowsill, the neglected daisies' petals have begun to wither.

Meg brought them out of obligation. You know this now. The daisies are there because the surgical pamphlet said it was 'necessary visual stimulation for a successful transition.' Meg hasn't been back to tend them. The last time you saw her, she didn't say she loved you.

You reach toward the daisies with a slowness you couldn't have fathomed in your flesh and bone body.

Your pace itself is a brand new form of camouflage.. The nurse doesn't seem to notice the dreamy uncoiling of leaves when she changes your IV. The doctor takes your vitals without mentioning it. As you continue to move, unnoticed and gloriously slow, courage swells through you. By the time you brush against the nearest flower, it is afternoon, and the daisies are tipping their faces toward the light.

Leaf to leaf, you connect. There is a sameness in the touch, a recognition, a swell of joy, and you imagine a garden stretching on forever, every flower delicate and identical in their quiet companionship.

Tenderly, you curl what was once your hand around the daisies. Together, you turn your faces to the sun.

SWINGS AND SUSPENSION

by D.A. Xiaolin Spires

Tingting throws the keychain at my head. The crinkly plastic-wrapped bauble bounces off my cheek, nosedives towards my torso and slides off my bulging belly. I catch it in my palm. "Sorry," she says, smirking. "Didn't mean to hit the baby bump."

I shake my head. She's about to be a mom and she still acts this silly.

I rub my thumb on the souvenir toy. Luminescent yellow, the color of the giant ball before me. A small round head. Except it has vertical slits, like the letter I for eyes and an O for a mouth, which is supposed to look like the number 101, but my eyes cross and it feels like some binary message making its way into my head.

The tour guide ignores our antics and continues on. "This 729-ton steel damper sways back and forth, a great marvel of a pendulum, held up by extremely thick cables of two thousand steel strands. The damper counteracts earthquakes and the gusty winds from typhoons acting on our magnificent Taipei 101. It keeps the building upright. There are two smaller dampers up in the spire, but this is the main one."

We all marvel at the giant ball before us, situated between the 88th and 92nd floors, a colossal sphere with such a momentous presence. It reminds me of when I was a kid and my mom took me abroad for the first time to Epcot Center. A giant geodesic sphere graced the landscape like a ship landing from beyond. It was covered in triangles, looking like the pineapples of my native Tainan in the south. This sphere, nestled in the iconic skyscraping symbol of Taiwan, had horizontal layers, rather than triangles.

"Looks kind of like terraces, like the oolong tea farms in the Maokong mountains," Tingting whispers to me, a little too loud.

The tour guide, who was in the midst of explaining something else, stops her spiel. Her grimace at being interrupted is hidden by a professional smile. "Yes, those steps you see," says the tour guide, "are the steel plates of increasing and then decreasing diameters that constitute the ball, layer by layer. Expert craftsmen welded them together."

"Ah," we say, marveling at the expertise of its production. I'm looking at the layers, from the top smallest one to the bulge in the middle of that ball and I feel my baby kick. I stare at the face of the alien-looking trinket of the mascot keychain in my hands, warped under its protective translucent plastic packaging. My baby kicks three more times, "one-oh-one" I think.

The floor begins to shake.

"Don't panic. Just get to the wall, away from the ledge," the tour guide says. She begins to herd us, waving her hands, flagging us over. We all move away from the gaping hole cut out from the center of the floor, containing the massive room-sized planet-like damper.

Tingting leads me as my legs shake. My knees ache as I proceed. The world leans and vertigo and chills sweep my body. My calves are already bloating; this shaking doesn't help my stability. I wipe cold sweat from my face with a sleeve. I imagine my fetus, sloshing around in amniotic fluid, just like this giant ball in the air that is supposed to sway.

But, the giant ball doesn't seem to be doing its job.

The baby kicks over and over as if yearning to get out. "Not yet," I say aloud. "We still have a few weeks!" Then I realize I'm talking to my belly and feel silly. But, no one is paying attention, as the tour crowd yaks in a frenzy, backed up against the wall. Heels and soles trying to grip onto the floor. Hands holding the wall, holding each other. Shouting and praying. A woman next to me starts to cry, tears streaming down her cheeks, rubbing rosary beads between her fingers.

The room sways in greater arcs now, first right, then left, and we slip about holding onto anything, placards, corners of walls, anything we could see, but the damper is strangely still. I'm transported, sitting on a swing set, a memory from when I was a child, eight years old, the sun streaming down my face, playing in the schoolyard, content. The bullies, Weichi and her lackeys, gathered around me, pushing me, faster and faster, taunting me, laughing. My hair flew, tangled and landed on my face as I oscillated back and forth. My breath stopped. I screamed. I fell off, landed in a sprawl, spraining my wrist. The bullies ran off, leaving me there. My lips bled into the dirt.

My lips are bleeding now, and I realize I'm biting them. And all I think is: *I want to get to that ball.* Taipei 101 is swaying, and people are holding on for dear life around me, hanging onto door handles. *Shake it!* But, it's a voice, an urging, not my own. It's coming from inside me. *Don't let them bully you!* I know I must be delirious, but I don't care, and I step towards the ball.

And something clicks in my head. *The wind. We must counteract the wind. We,* I think, wondering who I'm referring to.

"No!" I hear Tingting's yell behind me, but too late. I sprint, as fast as my aching calves allow, jump onto the ledge and spring off, flying through the air. I miraculously grab onto one of the terraces, my fingers clasping onto the edge of the bulky middle of the enormous sphere. The air feels cold here in the center of the room, or maybe it's just my body realizing I'm hanging off this cliff of a layer. Any false move and I plunge to my death. The ball leans and I'm trying to hold on. Strength fills my fingers and it's not me, as I feel the continuous kicks. It's my fetus projecting onto me, taking hold of my body. We had a donor sperm and now I'm wondering if the lab lied about the source. The doctor always had this wayward smile like she was hiding something. *Who is in there, in that belly of mine, controlling me? Tingting's genes or not? And who else?*

But, no time to ponder, I kick my feet but don't get any leverage. I struggle, my knuckles shaking. My fingers manage to pull my body up, though I've never done a single finger pushup in all my life. But it's strength from within and a will to live that fills me. Achingly, I climb to the top, ignoring the shouts my way.

And there, sitting at the pinnacle of the giant damper, my water breaks. Taipei 101's leaning left and then right, and I should be panicking, but I'm strangely calm. It's a birth that must be a world record and I struggle with underpants and before I even manage to peel off my skirt, she's out, along with the placenta. Still, the earth shakes, tremors that keep passing and still the tower careens this way and that. I see a face one-oh-one—vertical slit eyes and a circle mouth.

An alien face, the one from the trinket, the mascot of this building leering at me from my cradled arms. I stifle a scream, close my eyes and suck out amniotic liquid from her translucent nostrils. She breathes. From her skin, tiny mounds arise. Blue and green. I feel them nudging into my arms, against my goosebumps, emerging from the strangeness of it all. I bring her up to my eyes, her umbilical cord still dangling, and I see that on her forehead, on her nose bridge, cheeks, everywhere are little nubs, growing thinner, sharper and they start poking out of her skin, tall and straight, spires, many of them, until I can no longer deal with the pain and rip my skirt to stuff as a buffer. It works, for a bit. The screaming of Mandarin from the tour group stops echoing and falls to a mute, as I can no longer hear them, all I can focus on is my baby before me, shifting, transforming. I feel a heartbeat coming from under my rear, deep and sonorous, vibrating from the damper. Is that possible? *Thump thump thump.*

And my baby's arms reach out in jagged blue-green sleeves, not sleeves, but her arms, made of one giant spire with fractals of spires coming out of it. I smell a primordial dank musk and I realize the small spires are cutting my arms through the bandage of ripped skirt, slick in blood and amniotic fluid, but I dare not let her go. The spirals rising from her skin are four-sided and latticed, like the giant sky-piercing Taipei 101 building we are all in. Her arms lengthen, not mechanical like the extending arms of the bucket trucks that fix street lamps, but more organic, and she reaches out to two of the steel cables of the dampers. Her arms splay out like a snake, the latticed pattern of her skin so much like scales, and she grabs the cables holding the damper and begins to shake them. The damper sphere hiccups from under me, a jerky totter, as if realizing it had been still, derelict in its duties, and starts to swing, like it's supposed to do.

I move with it, swaying, like a pebble perched on a dancing turtle. I grab onto my daughter tighter, if I could call this monstrosity my daughter, as her arms go limp, sagging as she still holds onto the cables, her job done. I realize the screams have turned to awed mumbles.

Taipei 101, the building itself, stops lurching, stops shaking as much. My eyes can gauge that, even as the damper I am on careens one way and another.

I'm exhausted. I stare into my baby's vertical slit eyes, *one* and another *one*, as their immaturity encodes. I can't read the eyes like I can a regular human's, can't tell if they express happiness or fear, but something in my head says, *don't worry.* It feels mature, the voice of reason, of someone older than me, and I know she has saved us all, saved me from that feeling of helplessness when the bullies pushed me too fast, too fast—she swooped in and took all that fear away. She retracts her arms from the cables, letting the giant damper move on its own.

I'm swinging on the damper now, sitting at its apex, but I feel no fear, just a deep sense of love at this strange creature before me. Her eyes lizard-like and her scaled arms of blue-green glass wrapped around me a dozen times. Tingting's over in the mass, huddled with the other bodies, waiting for the tremors to stop, and I want to signal to her that yes, this is our kid—but I hear a gentle sigh and a soft gurgle from within my embrace, and I can't keep my eyes from the cute little ring of her mouth and the captivating coos emerging from her lips.

AMAZON

by Tori Cárdenas

My tattoo was of a budding flower. It was above my heart, over the scar where my left breast had been. It was a peony, pink and pale orange, like a perfect scoop of sherbet melting on an Albuquerque summer afternoon.

A lot of the women in my support group had tattoos over their scars, or around them, highlighting their beauty and their mystery, and providing a kind of pain that they felt invested in. They chose it, putting themselves on the fire to forge a new kind of beauty. This was the kind of woman I wanted to be—proud, fierce, and determined. All I could manage to stomach for a while was Jello, but that wasn't stopping me.

"Baby, you're an Amazon," Sebastian said, holding me in the hospital bed a few days after I woke up from surgery. "They used to cut off their breasts so that they could be more accurate with their bows on horseback. It was a sign of strength."

"They also didn't like men very much."

"But you like me, right? You're my Amazon."

Somehow, that didn't make me feel better. Very little made me feel better. Sleeping and not talking were two of those things. And bless his heart, but Sebastian didn't let me do enough of either. He insisted on keeping me up all day with activities and stupid dad-jokes.

⌒

Mastectomies aren't a fucking joke. After the surgery, my hair had all fallen out, even the delicate hairs on my arms, the stubble on my legs, my pubic hair, the one spiky hair that grew out of my right nipple. It was all gone. In a perfect world, one could achieve this level of hairlessness without the chemo, the radiation, the nausea, the tremors. In a perfect world, beauty would come at no cost. But this was the world where I got breast cancer at twenty-five. Beauty standards don't apply here.

In an effort to still feel beautiful, I replaced the breast with a tattoo, and all felt right with the world. Not right away. The pain returned with the poke and pinch and scrape of the tattoo machine, mimicking the pins and needles I had during the healing process from surgery. It was itchy. It peeled. New skin rippled in under the flaky skin and for a minute, it felt like the cancer all over again.

But it was gorgeous. Ready to bloom. Ready to make a fresh start. Normally, a bud is a herald of spring, fertility, new beginnings. But my tattoo was frozen in time and I was worried that I would grow impatient waiting for its petals to open up into a sunset of pinks and oranges. Time couldn't stand still like that forever, could it? Sebastian tried to convince me otherwise.

"Someday," he always told me. "It'll bloom."

Always, when he told me, I scoffed.

But yesterday, when I went to the doctor for a checkup and caught a glimpse of my tattoo in the vibrating fluorescent lights, the angle of the petals seemed to have shifted ever so slightly.

"You get more work done? It looks good," Dr. Martinez said. He had a few tattoos himself. "It looks like it's opening up…so realistic. Who's your artist?"

"Hayley Star," I said. Her shop was in the East Mountains, and she gave a discount to breast cancer survivors being a survivor herself. Recently, she was featured on a tattoo reality show and after that, women started coming from all over the country to meet her and sit in her chair; I was just lucky we lived in the same town.

"Well, color me impressed. I've never seen such photorealism before. I might send some more work her way. She's got a good thing going," he said as he examined the paperwork for my remaining breast. "Everything seems fine, Jo. We'll schedule you to come back next month, but until then, try to take it easy. I know you're a busy lady, but you need to rest, too."

I nodded but I wasn't really paying attention.

At home in the mirror, I looked at my tattoo more closely. Aside from looking slightly more opened, nothing about the peony had changed or shifted or faded. I pulled a loose shirt on, made a cup of lemonade, and fell asleep on my chair in the living room. The sunshine pouring in through the window was always enough to help me sleep. Even through the worst of the chemo. Even through the worst of Sebastian's snoring. But he wouldn't be home for a few hours yet. I had to take the chance to sleep when I could.

I slipped into a quiet dream about kayaking down the Rio Grande, something I hadn't done since I was diagnosed a little over a year ago. This was the first year I wouldn't be going. The first year since I was ten. But in my dream, everything was the same; the water was green and lazy and it was late afternoon, rays of light trickling over the edge of the mountain to my right. Insects buzzed across the surface of the water and the sun was cozy on my face and arms as I steered myself downriver.

"Jo! Josefina!" Sebastian. Sebastian was calling. But he wasn't standing on the banks of either side of the river. I opened my eyes, and there he was, his cold hand shaking my arm, warm from the sun. "Jo!"

"What do you want? Don't wake me up when I'm napping," I said. I don't like being woken up from naps. That's rule number one. "Your hands are freezing." Cold hands are number two.

"Jo, are you okay? How did your appointment go?"

"Leave me alone, Seb," I said. I wanted to go back to the river. "I was having a good dream." I folded my arms over my chest and yawned.

"Jo, take your shirt off."

"I'm not in the mood, Seb." I was awake all of a sudden. He hadn't ever said that to me.

"No, seriously, look at your tattoo," he pulled my shirt down slightly, even though I was sitting in the window, curtains wide open to the street outside. And there, under his fingers, the petals of my breast cancer peony tattoo were opening, stretching, spreading across the left side of my chest. Shades of pale rose, tangerine, cream, coral erupted in brilliant blends of color—more color than I had paid for. The veins in the petals were even more clearly defined, more than the tendrils they had been this morning. The green leaves were somehow greener, more vibrant, more alive, fuzzier with tattooed texture. This wasn't a $600 tattoo anymore. I didn't even want to think how much a tattoo this big and complex might cost.

My mouth hung open and I gasped for air.

"Get in the car," Seb said. "We'll go ask Hayley." He fumbled around looking for his keys, even though I assumed he'd just gotten home. That man would misplace his head if it weren't attached. I don't know how he has such a good memory for his work, but the brain is not something I claim to understand. I can't even comprehend less complex bodily functions fully. How I developed cancer in the first place is one of those things.

"They're in your hand, dummy. Let's go," I said, and I pulled on a hoodie. It was an early summer day, but I had goosebumps.

⌒

It took about twenty minutes to drive to Hayley's tattoo shop in Albuquerque's East Mountains, but it felt like an eternity. Golden Goddess Tattoo was part of a larger plaza that was mostly modern, with a cute café and a sleek bookstore full of cool, well-read teenagers working the counter. But the inside of Golden Goddess looked like an old curiosities shop, the mahogany-paneled walls covered from floor to ceiling by curio cabinets, tall canvases with slick oil-paint flowers and nude women, climbing philodendrons on hooks and glass domes covering dried roses and withered homunculi. A taxidermy moose head surveyed the shop from the back of the room, its long antlers draped with a string of orange Christmas lights.

Hayley was leaning against the glass countertop flipping through songs on the computer, the tattoos painted up and down her arms as varied and curious as the things collected in her shop.

"Hey girl, come on in," she smiled and called me over. "How'd your work heal up? Need any touch-ups?"

"It healed perfectly, I appreciate you asking. But what I really came in for was this," I walked over to her booth with her and pulled down my loose shirt.

"Looks great, what's wrong?"

I scrolled through the pictures on my phone, found the picture of the tattoo freshly done, and showed her. The tightly closed bud and the blooming flower on my chest now couldn't be more different, unless the colors were completely changed.

She froze. Then ran her long fingers over the tattoo, asking if it itched, tingled, peeled. But it hadn't. It was just...blooming, like a video playing on my skin in slow motion. Her gentle touch moved over and over the tattoo, as if she were feeling for a secret latch or lock or lump.

Finally, she sighed. "This isn't my work. I mean, I remember working with you, Jo. We talked about *My Favorite Murder* for three hours. And this looks like exactly like one of my peonies. But I didn't do that," she said. The stone plugs in her ears wagged as she shook her head.

"What do you mean you didn't do this? You were my artist, Hayley," I said. If the person who put this on my body didn't even understand where it came from, what else was I supposed to do?

"You could try asking your doctor. I really don't have any idea what's going on."

I felt fuzzy, the edges of my vision blurring and my stomach floated toward the ceiling. I collapsed into her tattoo chair and fainted.

⌒

When I woke, I was in a hospital bed. The room looked like the same room I had spent my healing time in after the surgery. I was probably at Lovelace. Sebastian wasn't around, but I had a nurse button and I called for another blanket. It was freezing, intentionally cold to keep the viruses at bay.

A peek under my scratchy hospital gown showed that my tattoo was still blooming, petals beginning to curl in toward the stem as the center began to reveal itself. Suddenly, I wasn't impatient anymore. My tattoo was changing beneath my top layer of skin, the top layer of my attention. What would happen when the bloom's brilliant pinks and oranges began to turn brown? I decided I didn't really want to know.

When Sebastian came back, I said, "I want to go home."

He sat down in the vinyl-upholstered visitor's chair. It was a nauseating mauve. I couldn't stand to look at it. I felt dizzy.

He said, "The doctor is coming back in to see you soon. They sent away for blood tests. I think we ought to wait."

But I didn't want to spend any more time in this hospital. I wanted to fall asleep in my window at home and dream of the river.

A QUICK GETAWAY

by Sherri Cook Woosley

Randy drives the curves of the backroad like we're on the Scrambler, the ride he works at the carnival. As he crosses over the median, hand loose on the wheel, I want to tell him to slow down, but I don't want him to think I'm a nag or he might not take me with him when the carnival leaves. He's not a great catch, but maybe I'm not either so I don't say anything when he slings an arm across my shoulder and his hand dangles too close to my chest. Foster kids don't get anything for free.

We pass a field of dry corn stalks and then a weathered wooden fence appears, running parallel to the road. The posted sign reads *Don't pick the fruit*. Randy pulls the truck over to the side, tires sinking in the grass.

"What's this?" he asks, his gaze wandering over pruned trees planted in straight lines. Golden peaches hang from low branches, begging to be picked. It's late August, the tail end of peach season.

"I've never been back here," I say. It's true. I've been with this foster family for almost a year and during that time I've worked on the farm and gone to the local high school. The carnival this week is my first opportunity to escape the unbearable loneliness.

"I'm getting one," Randy announces. His hand hovers over the ignition key, but he leaves the truck running. Instead, he moves the hand from my shoulder to my thigh, right where my cut-offs end, and squeezes. "Be ready for a quick getaway."

He laughs, but I don't. I do want a quick getaway. I want to leave a rural school where I'm the weird kid who likes to draw and has a tattoo of wings on my left bicep. I want to leave a foster family who only needs a warm body to feed and water the sheep. I want to leave a farm where they name and then kill their animals. I asked if I could plant a garden instead. They thought it was a joke.

Randy climbs the fence and then wanders, caressing the fuzz of one peach and then reaching for another. When he ducks under a branch and moves deeper into the orchard, I can't see him anymore. I look at the keys in the ignition, the air conditioner pumping stale air around the truck cabin. It smells like cigarette smoke and the sickly sweet lemonade they sell at the carnival. For a moment I imagine sliding behind the wheel, but there's no point in driving away because I would be as lonely as I am now.

A sudden breeze brings the scent of ripe peaches through the window. The rustling of the nearby cornstalks could be whispers, encouraging me to get out of the truck. Overhead, the sky is the special blue that promises Autumn is coming. My mouth waters for fruit, for eternal summer, and I choose to climb the fence, too.

I'm greeted by a single wasp flying toward my face and then veering away. Like Randy, I wander deeper into the orchard. Each of the trees is perfect, the green leaves not touched with a hint of gold or red. The fourth tree in, I stop. My hand curves around a fruit so soft and delicate that the skin yields to my touch. I don't grab or twist; the peach falls into my hand. Through a crack in the skin a drop of juice rolls down the back of my hand. On instinct, I lick it. An immediate tingle begins on my tongue. The juice is difficult to describe because it's sweet, but not like the carnival lemonade. I keep the droplet on my tongue, savoring, and then press my tongue to the roof of my mouth, crushing the droplet so that the liquid coats the sides of my tongue. I shudder in pleasure.

The air vibrates with the movement of hundreds of wings. I peer around the leaves, looking for the orchard's inhabitants.

Swoosh! The branches part and Randy is there, his face smeared with peach juice. "Take as much as you want," he says, laughing, gesturing like he owns this place.

We've made a mistake. I clench my fists until the nails dig into my skin because there's something foster kids learn early. Head to the bed with the broken frame and the thinnest blanket. The nice bed is already taken. You set your garbage bag of stuff in front of that one and you're gonna get jumped. Your fault for thinking you're somebody. And this place is so nice, it belongs to someone. Hell, there was even a sign.

Randy grabs a peach off the tree, yanking with a rough motion so that leaves come off too, and he shoves the fruit into his mouth. Hands free, Randy yanks his shirt over his head and tosses it to the grass. He pulls the peach from his mouth and smears the fruit all over his chest.

"Lick it off."

I shake my head. His eyes frighten me. I've seen men drunk before, but never on peaches. I don't question it though, don't try to rationalize fermented fruit. I listen to my instincts and they say to run.

"Ow." Randy's hand claps to his shoulder. "Something stung me."

He moves his hand and a wasp falls to the grass. We stare at the live insect, a shiny black color, elegant abdomen, jointed antennae broken. The fruit droplet still in my mouth tingles. Randy stoops down and I know what he's going to do.

"Don't hurt her," I say, my words thick as I speak around the fruit juice on my tongue. "Please. She's beautiful."

"She?"

"Only female wasps have stingers," I say, embarrassed at the look he gives me. "Their stingers aren't barbed so they can sting again and again."

Randy crushes the insect between his index finger and thumb. "How's that, Ms. Science?" he asks as he wipes the remains on his jeans.

Buuuzzzzzzz.

Before either Randy or I can run, the wasps arrive. They fly past us in a living black cloud and come together into the shape of a woman with a tiny waist and antennae. My heart quivers at the alien beauty. They are all female, dangerous and full of righteous anger.

"You trespassed." The wasps work together so that it looks like their mouth speaks. The voice is many voices. "You ate our fruit." The woman-shape quivers with rage. "And then you killed one of us."

Randy's eyes go wide, but then he laughs. "Un-be-lievable." He lurches forward, fist cocked, and punches. The wasp woman dissolves into individuals, unhurt by his clumsy swing.

The insects surround Randy. He twists, batting his hands, but can't avoid the coordinated attack. Maybe I should feel horror, but instead I watch in fascination as his skin tightens to leather, his eyes darken, and his body shrinks. The transformation is like flipping the pages of a sketch pad quickly to make art dance into life. Randy folds in on himself until he is the size of the other wasps, but he is different. His body is yellow with red stripes, like a warning. He staggers on the orchard ground trying to work the jointed legs. One black wasp hovers in the air above him.

The rest of the wasps reform the queen, the bodies working together in practiced efficiency. Their face watches and they cross their arms over their chest.

Still on the ground, Randy's wings flutter. The hovering wasp will kill him. I would have known this even if the queen's anger didn't burn the air, even if the drop of juice didn't tingle on my tongue. Maybe the hovering wasp is next of kin or maybe this is her job within the colony.

I'm going to receive a punishment next and I only have this moment to make a decision. I remember the keys in the truck, Randy's advice about a quick getaway. I remember his hand dangling near my chest and then on my thigh, the way he shoved the peaches into his mouth and then smashed the female wasp. I keep these images in my head as I fall to my knees on the ground and scoop up Randy's new body. I hold him between my finger and thumb. His surprise turns to anger. I feel it through the juice on my tongue. His abdomen pumps repeatedly against the flesh of my thumb, but nothing happens. I told him only females have stingers. I could have explained that the stinger developed from the ovipositor, the organ for egg-laying. I squeeze. There is a crunch of exoskeleton, audible over the omnipresent buzzing. I drop his dead body into the grass and look up at the queen to see if she will accept my apology.

The queen dissolves into disorder, wasps flying ellipticals and returning, a conference, and then they reform into the quiet of consensus.

The queen accuses me. "You are still a peach thief."

Yes, my tongue is still covered with the stolen juice. I walk forward on my knees into the queen, quivering with fear and hope, and I open my mouth to the wasps. For three heartbeats there is no reaction. Then they are on my face, feet on my tongue, buzzing filling my ears, and my flesh is surrounded by the insects. Tingling, same as on my tongue, spreads from the crown of my head to my toes. I am vulnerable and exposed, intimate with the wasps in a way I'd never imagined. They know me in a way that no foster family ever has.

And then it's over. They have taken back their juice and I no longer have a connection to this garden. The absence aches like a missing limb.

"We accept your penance," the queen says, in their multi-voice. "You may leave now."

I look at the impossible blue sky, the green leaves, the wild beauty. I breathe in sun-ripened peaches. Then I look at the queen and press my hands together. If they know me, then they know what I will ask.

"But can I stay?" I throw open my arms, welcoming the pain if it means I will finally belong. "Sting me."

THE QUEENS' SECRET

by H.L. Fullerton

The divine right of kings is nothing compared to the queens' secret. Like honey to hieroglyphs. Ask any pharaoh.

⌣

Seth still felt the sting of Becky's leaving. It's why he let the hornet move into his workshop. Becky was allergic; panicked at the merest *tzz* despite her omnipresent Epi-Pen. It was sort of amazing she hadn't left him sooner. They lived on an orchard, for christsake—a honeybee nirvana and, come apple-picking time, a veritable wasp feast.

If only he'd checked the apples. He knew wasps bored into fruit to gorge themselves on the sugary flesh. Usually he inspected each piece. The one time he didn't... Becky freaked when she discovered the hole in the McIntosh. No wasps were inside, but the damage had been done.

Maybe if he'd agreed to move—but no, he'd lived here all his life. His business was here, his family. Just not his wife. Who would've made him smoke the entire orchard if she'd caught sight of the yellow and black banded hornet now exploring his collection of poplar trim. It was a miracle this wasp queen hadn't succumbed to last summer's vespine pogroms. (Despite their appearance, hornets weren't bees; they were wasps. Territorial, *aggressive* wasps.)

At first, it seemed apropos to watch the hornet build her nest while his life was falling apart. By late summer, he didn't have the energy to destroy her masterpiece. Becky's abandonment took its toll on his health—physical and mental.

⌒

Ancient Egyptians and their cats. It's not what everyone thinks. Cats can't stave off death. That nine lives bullshit was made up by a Persian, maybe a stone-chewing Sumerian. The Egyptians wrapped *their dead.*

⌒

If Becky really loved him, she would've stayed. For better or worse, wasn't that how it went? Seth watched the hornet build her nest, mouthful by mouthful. He marveled at the colorful striations, from the pale bands of birch to golden rings of oak, the reddish swirl of apple married to muddy maple—and thought about what devotion really meant.

⌒

Wrapped their god-kings in strips of linen, layer upon layer, held in place with resin. They would have wrapped themselves in paper if they could've—but they didn't know the secret of the queens. So flax had to do.

⌒

The hornet watched Seth back. This man-drone smelled like trees. He made things out of wood. He let her be.

⌒

Resin, for the unenlightened, is tree sap. Because people can't chew bark and spit out pulp. Who do you think made the Egyptians' precious papyri?

⌒

Seth wasn't sure when he began calling the hornet Becky. Probably about the time his vision started blurring. Maybe the day he looked down on his arm to find a dozen hornets—Becky's daughters—nibbling on his perpetually dry skin. He couldn't feel them, knew that was a sign he wasn't eating properly, but couldn't make himself care. "Bet if we'd had kids, you woulda stayed," he mumbled and sounded a little drunk, even though he hadn't touched a drop.

⌒

They washed the corpse in wine—fermented fruit—and scented it with cassia and cinnamon—tree barks. Packed it in natron, thinking salts might turn dead skin papery thin. It didn't.

⌒

Thirsty. Seth's mouth felt packed with sawdust. He reached for his mug. When was the last time he'd checked his insulin pump? Something buzzed near his ear. His arms waved, flailed. He imagined he saw the hornet queen's heart-shaped face, antennae arched in concern, hover before him. "Becky," he whispered, then collapsed onto his workbench.

⌒

The wetyr hollowed out the body but returned the heart: the only chambered organ; four snug little homes for the afterlife. Beeswax was used to seal the body shut: mouth, ears, nose, the embalmer's mark. Still think the Egyptians worshiped felines above all else?

⌒

The hornet queen danced around the man-drone, ambled up his cheek. Outside, her daughters, her little queens readied for their nuptial flight. Her drones preened in the midsummer sun and chased. But their agitated motions didn't draw her as the man-drone's did.

His wind-breath smelled of fruit. He dipped and twitched; fell into the almost death. Ravenous, she burrowed into him as if he were an apple. He tasted sweeter than oak sap. She called to her children and they supped on the strange, cumbersome fruit.

⌒

Mimicking vespine combs, the ancients placed their mummies— thrice bundled—in nestled wooden coffins, then a stone sarcophagus, then a tomb.

⌒

The grist worked all autumn to wrap their queen's hollowed-out lover. If Seth could see his paper shroud, it would remind him of a tree stump mottled with burls. But he saw nothing, knew nothing. Something sticky seeped from his sightless eyes. His nose and ears were plugged. His bandaged jaw gaped; hornets flew in and out his mouth. Occasionally, his face pressed tight against his wrappings, a strained ripple on an otherwise still pond. His heart—now the king's chambers—thrummed strangely. It pulsed with life, but not his own. Nestled deep within the man he once was were Becky and her three special eggs. *Seth's daughters.*

He felt the vibration of the grist as they lovingly built their new kingdom; sensed his queen's commands but was unable to respond—not yet.

⌒

The Egyptians waited for their dead to walk, but they never did. Because only the queen of queens knows the secret of the wandering hive. Only her love-sting can wake the dead.

SHE SHELLS
by Eden Royce

Auntie Talika molts once a year and needs a safe place to hide, to heal, before she ventures out into the cold waters again. She usually spends this time—about a month, sometimes more—with me. It is the only time I ever see her anymore.

I run my fingers through her hair, removing the tangles formed as she thrashed and flailed to free herself of her old body, which lies next to her on the floor of my conservatory.

I resist the urge to nudge her thin, translucent carapace away from me while I tend to her hair. A replica of my aunt in gossamer, face upturned toward me, toward the light; it unsettles me, even after seeing it countless times. Sunlight reflects off the face of her discarded shellskin, making the mouth look as though it's smirking at me. The back has been torn open, clawed out from the inside, and the ridges of the tear blossom open like sharp-edged petals.

My fingers retain the slick slip of the candlenut butter and peach oil I use on her tresses. I rub my hands together, awed at how different they feel, how much softer. Like auntie's new body, grub soft, and giving. It's also grub white and I know she hates to see herself this way. She won't look into a mirror or the clear sea until her cells release color, first in tiny irregular circles, covering her body in faux freckles, then spreading into a uniform shade of deep brown. Then, it will harden into her new shellskin.

Then she will leave.

But for now, I take care of her.

I tug too hard on her braid and she hisses, baring sharp pointed teeth set between bruise purple lips. I know from experience her uncovered flesh is sensitive to even the slightest pressure. I swallow my sigh. My hands gentle against her scalp, the only apology I will offer.

"Talika," I ask. She doesn't like for me to call her by her title of Auntie. "Did my mother ever comb my hair?"

"Yessss…" Her words come out on a sputter of breath. "Many, many timessss."

"Tell me… I want to remember."

My auntie's lisp forms the words to a tale about my mother and I am drawn in. Into a memory that somehow belongs to all the ancestors, yet is still mine alone. A story of scales and snakes and stone. One of sisters, before meddling gods begat troublesome daughters. I stiffen at the tale. Myths are never kind, but reality is far crueler.

While she speaks, I smooth my palms over her plaits and conjure a memory of my own. I was voted festival queen when I was fifteen, due to receive a crown and sash and all the customary regalia fitting of such a title. Even had a local seamstress sew me a dress. Auntie broke my arm off at the elbow joint three days before the ceremony. Threw it into the back garden for the birds to tear apart.

"Rely on your brain, dear. Not your looksss," she said. "Don't be like your mother."

My arm grew back, of course, but it took the rest of the summer and I stayed indoors hiding from the other children.

Auntie called the seamstress and had her put long sleeves on the dress, paying the woman extra for her trouble. But I never wore it. Eventually moths ate holes in the gauzy fabric and I ripped it into shreds. One of those shreds was near my hand, a scrap I dusted with, the glimmer of the cloth long gone. How easy would it be to twirl it around auntie's neck?

My hands curl into fists.

"I'm going to bed. Can I get you anything before I go?" My every cell oozes with the insincerity of my words. "Food or drink?"

"No, thank you," she says, breaking off a piece of her old exoskeleton and shoving it between her lips.

I turn and leave the room, flee from the sound of teeth on bone.

Upstairs, I wipe my oiled hands up and down my arms, feeling the small ridge where my new arm sprouted. It aches sometimes, when storms hover over the sea. Funny how the ache grows after each molt.

Sleep doesn't come. Thirst does, along with the desire for this month to pass quickly. I tiptoe downstairs, intent on filling a glass with dark wine.

Hot sobs echo off the glass walls of the conservatory, condensing against the glass and running in rivulets down its surface. I ease closer on my human-like feet, silent.

Auntie Talika's segmented body now lies in a shallow pool of tears. Her abandoned shellskin, half-eaten, is floating far out of reach across the room. The molt makes not only her body tender, but her soul. I approach with care, dipping my hand in her tears to moisten it before I place it on her new-skin shoulder.

Unbidden, I remember the day my mother died. Talika held me as I cried, her mouth parts clicking soft reassurances. Her tongue touched my tears, taking them into herself, while she rocked me against her chest. I fell asleep to the sound of her heartbeat, the sound of ocean waves. There were no words to comfort me and she gave me none.

"I'm sssorry I couldn't keep her alive forever," she cries. "Your mother wasss much better than me. Your mother would have been kinder, gentler. You needed—" Her words ebb away like tides.

I kneel in the soft saltwater and pull her to my own breast. I offer her no words, because there are none. I hold her gently, the only acceptance of her apology I can give. We weep together silently, filling the conservatory with tears, our hearts thumping the beat of the sea.

RAVEN HEARTS

by Stephanie Herman

Raven hearts are too small to grieve. It's an inevitability of physics; if their hearts grew too full, their wings couldn't hold them aloft. Not enough surface area, too little lift. So they shed their grief upon liftoff, leaving it draped across branches and telephone poles like dull, diaphanous snakeskin.

Two ravens watch you from the warped peak of the collapsing barn, stark ink against the fogged sky. Behind you the house sits empty of all but memory and sympathetic casseroles. The rains have passed and the air lies still, heavy with moisture and the scent of earth. The only sounds are the squelch of mud beneath your feet and the occasional husky murmur from the birds.

You envy them. Land-bound, there's no reason your heart shouldn't weigh you down.

Not like a raven's heart.

Proportionately, birds have larger hearts than mammals, to move more blood. Carry more oxygen. Keep their muscles working and their bodies airborne. But ravens are lighter than they look. Less dense. An adult raven has a four-foot wingspan, yet weighs less than the eight-week-old kitten you adopted last January. The one that died under the wheels of a Subaru three months later. The one that is lodged somewhere in your left ventricle.

As you approach, the ravens tilt their heads to get a better look. What do you look like to them today, wearing black on black on black like they do? What catches their attention? Perhaps it is the flash of the silver buttons bisecting your blouse, or the mirror shine of your boots where the mud hasn't yet covered. Perhaps it is the gleaming length of the rifle in the crook of your arm.

Or maybe it isn't the glint at all.

Once, you saw a documentary all about ravens; how they recognize faces, how they use tools. One bird dropped rocks into a vase, raising the water level until it could reach a floating bit of food. Another pushed the right buttons in the right order after observing what its fellow did to earn its treat.

So maybe they can tell something else is different about you today. Maybe they watch you because you are watching them.

You think in order to be so smart, ravens must have traded some of their heart-space for head-space. It's what you would do. What you tried to do during grad school, when you started falling asleep in your study cube at the library so you wouldn't have to go home to an empty house.

Or rather, to the empty house that reminded you of your mother, who said, "Why do you waste your time with so much school? That will never make you happy. Not like kids."

She died before you could make her proud, or prove her wrong. If you listen carefully, you can hear the echoes of her voice caught in your superior vena cava. Nothing dulls those echoes, not even tenure and publications and the growing weight of your name.

The barn is close now. Any closer and you'll lose sight of the birds. You circle to find the best position, heedless of the mud splashing up your boots and splattering the hem of your skirt. The birds stretch their wings and flare their diamond-shaped tails, turning to keep you in sight the entire way.

You read somewhere that ravens mate for life. Maybe it's just easier to survive in pairs, but you like to think they fall in love. You only ever see two together, so certainly they have no patience for friends or cousins or overgrown children. Not like crows, with their boisterous mobs. That's fine. You've never needed or wanted a crowd.

But of everything packed in your heart, you wouldn't mind remembering Ravi. How he took twice as long as you to get ready in the morning. His obsession with stupid pug memes. The way he'd run to the corner store to get you Oreos when you had a particularly hard day at work. How he filled up the house with his rickety hand-made furniture. How he had filled it the rest of the way with his half-read books and socks and smile.

You plant your feet and check the safety on the rifle.

The feel of Ravi's arm around you when you fell asleep each night. The way he looked in the hospital bed. In the coffin.

Take aim.

Ravi, clogging up your heart and blocking the flow of blood. Of oxygen.

The shot shatters the air and bounds across the field. A squalling black-feathered body bursts into the sky. The other tumbles down the roof and lands at your feet. You kneel.

When you were young, you helped your father tend a small flock of sheep in this barn. He always brought the pregnant ewes in well before they were due. He'd seen a raven kill a newborn lamb while its partner distracted the mother. They'd known she was pregnant. They'd stalked her for days, waiting for the birth and then taking what they'd needed.

The blood on your fingers is warm, the tiny heart slick and still trembling with electrical impulses. So light it barely presses against your palm.

You heard once that ravens roll seabird chicks off cliffs to avoid drawn out battles with their parents. They gather to the sounds of gunshots and wolf packs, stealing kills and eating the carrion left behind. They are survivors.

You draw the knife across your chest and reach between your ribs. Your congested heart flickers against your fingers like a dying florescent light.

You are a survivor too.

HER BLOOD LIKE RUBIES IN THE GROUND

by Eugenia M. Triantafyllou

He finds the scarecrow girl sitting at the kitchen table, too small for the chair, feet dangling as she drinks her milk in small sips. She watches Gunnar as he moves towards the coffee machine, or at least he thinks she does.

"Hello," she says blithely.

The hairs on the back of his neck prickle. He pours himself a cup of coffee. Then he turns around and rests against the counter.

Her hair is blades of wheat, her eyes two flat stones. The left one has a jigsaw bit missing on the side. He can't stop staring at it. Her face is covered in dirt from the field, yet her white dress is impeccable.

"Hello Anja," he mutters. *Hello scarecrow girl.*

Somewhere in the back of the house he hears the shower running. He imagines Margareta, naked, covered in weeds and mud, finally happy that their daughter is home.

She did a good job this year.

Last year the eyes were two buttons from Margareta's coat and the girl's lips were made with chicken bones from last night's dinner. It was uncanny to see them open and close; it made his stomach churn.

Not all of her is made of trinkets though. Some of her is flesh, or what feels and smells like flesh. The parts that come from her mother's blood. The parts that are not real are his. The absence of his blood, the unwillingness to raise the scarecrow girl this time every year.

"Can you make her porridge to eat?" Margareta's voice brings him back.

She stands by the kitchen door wearing one of his too-big shirts. Her black hair crawls like a glistening snake on her right shoulder.

"Her mouth looks... real this time," he begins to say. He doesn't know what else he can offer. What compliment is appropriate?

The girl flashes a wide smile over her cup of milk. Two lines of small teeth interrupted by a gap in the middle.

Her mouth looks exactly like Anja's on the days when she could still smile. Before the sickness.

⌢

Margareta and Anja spend the day playing and laughing, while Gunnar watches them protectively. Margareta never lets Anja leave the house, smell the summer in the air. She is afraid her daughter will leave her for the crops too soon, before her day is over.

The girl is not close to Gunnar and God knows they were close when Anja—the real Anja—was alive. But the scarecrow girl has only her mother's blood in her, the blood Margareta shed on that field of wheat. And with it goes Margareta's memories of Anja. The bond between them unbreakable.

"Why can't you do this for me?" Margareta said the first time before she went out into the fields barefoot and holding a basket of knickknacks. It was the anniversary of Anja's death.

He tried to explain that he too longed for Anja's golden hair, her eyes, her loud laughter. But he wasn't going to feed his blood to the dirt and make a scarecrow out of his own daughter. Even if the thing *looked* human.

Margareta left him in the house that night, black wisps of hair blowing in the wind and before morning she had her first Anja.

The day goes by and with it Anja's luster and life force. Margareta's initial joy wanes too and soon she sits on the recliner lethargic, empty. Like the day they came back from the hospital.

She begins to doze off and soon she falls into a deep slumber.

Anja is by her side, watching her in a tranquil, almost content way. Now that Margareta is asleep Anja looks less real. As if Margareta was making up for what the girl was missing.

Gunnar approaches Anja. He rests his hand on the wheat blades.

The scarecrow girl turns to look at him.

"Shall we?" he says.

The scarecrow girl nods and gets up. He takes her warm hand and leads her outside the house.

The sun is setting and they both walk slowly in the breezy summer night. The wind makes hollow sounds passing through the girl's hair.

She has Anja's shape and the gait of a little girl without a care in the world.

They are almost there now. At the spot where Margareta conjured Anja this morning.

There is a shallow hole in the ground.

"You can rest now," he says.

Suddenly, the girl turns around and hugs him. Her head rests softly against him. Her hair doesn't feel like blades. Gunnar wants to push her, to fight back, but his hands stay pinned on his sides.

"Good night, daddy."

"Good night, sweetheart," he replies. He squeezes Anja's shoulder a little longer than he intended to. "Sleep well."

He leaves. Now the empty space in his chest feels bigger. As if a bit of his heart was left behind. He wonders if that's enough for Margareta to make Anja whole next year.

EDGES OF LOVE
by G.D. Watry

I'm plucked from the ceaseless ocean, the warm basin of the unconscious universe.

My body is a soup of cells.

Formless.

Roiling and toiling in a bathysphere.

Then, a sensation like centrifugal force.

From an effervescent center, a whorl pulls together my elements in a chemical tilt-a-whirl. Atoms coalesce in miniature electrical storms. Greasy fats and watery proteins spin off my replicant genome. I'm a biological twister of cells multiplying and multiplying and multiplying. Bone wraps itself in muscle wraps itself in skin.

I float in the viscous ick. Separate. No longer one.

My world is embodied darkness, my limbs and curves perimeters, boundaries and borders.

A break in the union leads to cognitive dissonance, a murmur beyond awareness.

I.

So sure of I.

And here I feel an ache I'll come to know as pain. For as existence infects the mind, beautiful silence loses its claim.

⌒

You call me by the name of someone who's dead, your stern eyes on me in the rearview mirror. Your stiff jaw is tilted towards your chest.

Your skin runs tight over your high cheekbones. Lumpy shoulders poke through your black wool sweater like an oversized coat hangar.

I wonder if you've eaten. If we'll both learn how together.

The tube bustles with commuter traffic. It's part of a network that zigzags through the city like a technological spiderweb. Our auto-cab glides above magnetic tracks, careening around bends and climbing hills.

You say you're my mother. That's you're so happy I'm back, and that you can't wait to take me home.

"Your room is just the way you like it," you say. "It'll be like you never left."

In the backseat, I crack my knuckles, testing their durability.

"It'll be like you never left."

Outside, the polluted atmosphere flushes the sunset sky with aurora-like rays. My birthplace disappears into the city skyline, set aglow with bright neon. Billboards project through the evening haze.

A holo-ad shows a family gathered around a hospital bed. The mother lies sick, her family watching her final moments. Tears stream down their faces. "What if you didn't have to say goodbye?" bubbling words ask. The scene morphs, the projected pixels rearranging to form a scene depicting the same family around a table. The mother sits center, her face vibrant and beaming. Her family looks on at her affectionately. "You'll never be able to tell the difference," the text reads.

I whisper *his* name to myself.

You roll down the cab's back window, allowing the sterile air to tousle my hair. Laughing, I rise towards the enticing sensation, ticklish prickles against my scalp. But before I get too close, you roll the window up, cutting off the flow.

"Tsk-tsk-tsk," you say. "We don't want you tumbling out."

A stuffy atmosphere emerges, the scent of leather thick in the interior.

I tighten my seatbelt around my waist. So sure you're so sure of the world.

"It'll be different this time," you mutter. "I'll keep you safe forever."

⌢

Silver spires glisten in the dank moonlight like fluorescent fungi on a foggy bank.

I'm enraptured with the scene.

Eventually, you peel me away from the bedroom window. Your arm wrapped around my shoulders, you guide me to a wooden chest set at the foot of a twin poster bed. *His* name—my name—is blazoned on the chest in bright block letters.

"Open it," you say, anticipation overflowing in your voice.

A creaky lid lifts and I'm inside, my arms swallowed by the darkness of an unknowable past. It feels soft and loving.

There's an expectation from you. I feel that too.

But the stuffed things mean nothing to me.

In under an hour, you're in the living room arguing with customer service by phone.

"The memories aren't there," you say.

You never yell, but your tone is harsh, chiding and demeaning with assuredness in your insults.

"I didn't see that addendum in the contract," you say. "Yes, I read it carefully. Are you suggesting I don't read the contracts I sign carefully?"

Knees hugged to my chest, I rock to and fro in the hallway's darkness.

A portrait on the wall shows a much younger you and him. I feel his features on my face. They're a prison like language.

You're nothing but a flawed copy, a splintered part of me says. *A skipping bodily record.*

⌒

They offer a replacement. You decline, saying you no longer get your hopes up for disappointment. You don't return me either. "I'll make it work," you say before signing off. For this I'm grateful. I'm clinging to *this*. Whatever *this* is.

We try to find commonality in his interests. We color with oil pastels, tinkle piano keys in a hodgepodge duet and deliberate over a jigsaw puzzle of Neuschwanstein Castle.

I'm stuck on the sky and can't find three edge pieces.

You're stuck on the puzzle box's cover. Your eyes glassy, your lower lip sucked into your mouth.

"The gift shop was so out of place," you say, bringing a halt to my search. "There we were in this ornate castle in Bavaria with its glistening mosaic floors and gold-splashed furnishings. He was so fascinated by the frescoes and intricate wood carvings. He wanted to move there, talked about where he'd put all his toys. I can still hear his hustled steps echoing off the walls. It was so timeless and so fleeting. Then right at the end, a gift shop. Out of all the trinkets, he wanted the puzzle. So I got him the puzzle."

The touch of another still new, I reach out to you.

And suddenly, I feel that union. The glue that binds the universe.

"We'll make it work," I say, my soft hand atop your wrinkled one.

You look at me as if I'm new, a shy smile creeping up your cheeks. You nod, exhaling a rocky sigh.

We return to the puzzle pieces scattered across the floor.

I find a piece of the edge.

It feels so thin in my grip.

DISCARDED SKINS

by Steve Toase

The scent of aftershave stopped at the sea edge, no oak-leaves or moss able to survive the drenched cloying rot of the sea. Margaret kicked through the sand, disturbing a freshly cleaved crab leg.

Eight tides had scrubbed the beach since Spiri left. No trace of his footprints to show where he walked into the fret. Whatever called him back was not the sea.

Their romance had not been larceny. Margaret had not stolen his skin from chalk rocks like some washing-line thief. He had folded his foam-encrusted pelt, dried over paint flaked radiators, then vacuum-packed and slid below the bed they shared. Stowed like cargo beside her drysuit. Claimed residence of the house. Claimed residence in her arms.

Of course, he went back to the waves once a year for the gathering, when barks echoed like the cries of drowned fishermen. But they were creatures of two worlds, Spiri and his kin, and for him the call of the Marram grass and cliffs pulled stronger than the tide.

He had been gone four days and the gathering was still six months away.

Moving old paint tins and gardening tools, Margaret rooted about in the back of the shed for her scuba tanks. Back in the house, she reached under the bed for her own swimming skin, the neoprene padding dry for too long. Her hand brushed the empty vacuum pack and a gasp of wet fur erupted. She stopped for a moment and rested her head against the mattress.

⌒

Spiri's scent was even gone from the beach now. He could have returned to the sea out of choice, of course. Felt the call of pressure against his skin. The taste of salt and krill upon his tongue.

"I have swum into coves on distant beaches, and danced with blind fish far below the hulls of boats. I have eaten the finest urchins from amongst forests of coral, and I have no desire to live under the surface any more. I want to see the seasons change, and dance through the leaves in Autumn. Taste snow and whiskey to the sound of songs played on instruments older than the hands holding them. I am sick of the cloying cold of the water and the silt that hides the dead."

Margaret walked into the waves as if she had left her own clothes in a pile for a loved one to find. Even through the drysuit, the cold lapped up her skin, kelp and bladderwrack creasing past in the waltz of the currents.

Four more nights she searched the bay, the harbour, each day driving to the dive shop in town to fill the tanks once more. On the fifth night she swam the water below the cliffs where the vast fibre-optic tentacle slid under the surface, bringing conversations and porn through the ocean.

They fringed the cable, teeth clasped into the insulation. Their pelts were threadbare and scorched, tails swaying silt from the sea floor, splinters of seashells rising in plumes. She needed to see his eyes. Look into his face to know him. Mud filmed her diving mask, and she saw nothing but the dirt of the sea.

Margaret ran a finger across the glass. Her skin was old and slack on her bones. Not for the first time she wished she could detach it as Spiri did. Shed her flesh to start again and walk under different skies.

⌒

The fishermen knew her. They'd known her husband, Karl. Shouldered his coffin into the chapel. Made sure the cheques arrived from the widow fund every month. Some had tried to tempt her into drunkenness, and into bed, but she could out-drink them, and out-think them. After the first turned up with shattered knees, and no way to feed his family anymore, none of the other predators hunted her affections. They knew Spiri, and though they did not speak to him in case his kin sung them down through the waves, they did not disapprove.

Margaret walked into the bar and shrugged off her coat, beads of rain staining the uneven wooden floorboards. No-one looked up.

She pulled a chair toward her, sat down and pushed the envelope across the table. Bill looked up, sipped the last of his whiskey, and held the glass out to her. By the time she returned from the bar, the envelope had gone.

"What makes you think I can get this for you?" He turned the glass around. She tried not to stare at the tattoo on his arm, and the ragged cut where the surgeon's knife had taken his hand.

"Karl crewed your boat for ten years. I know you weren't just netting fish out there, and with Larne across the sea I know what you were hiding under the packing ice wasn't just Lebanese red."

"You know, do you?"

"If I was going to let slip, I would have done it by now."

Bill sipped his whiskey and closed his eyes.

"I don't need to know what you want this for."

Margaret stood up.

"That's good, because I'm not going to tell you."

⌢

Three days later the crate was in her shed, planks reeking of salt and dead cod. She cleaved off the top and lifted out a satchel, the olive green of the sky. Undoing the buckle, she checked each black, plastic-wrapped block, letters printed on in yellow telling her things she did not need to know. Fastening the bag once more, she sat on the crate and wept.

⌢

When the doorbell rang she thought it was Spiri returned to climb into her bed. Then the police to bury her in granite far from the coast.

"Can I come in?"

Bill stood on the doorstep, wrist cupped in hand.

She nodded and stood aside as he ducked to avoid the lintel. While the kettle boiled, she watched him stare at the photo on the mantelpiece. All five of the crew stood in front of the boat, his arm still intact.

She passed him the cup and he nodded thanks.

"Can I help?" he said after a pause, steam smearing his glasses.

Margaret shook her head.

"Whatever it is, it can't be that bad."

She pictured Spiri's kin welded to the undersea cable, their canine teeth sheered through the insulation, eyes rolled back in their heads.

"It can."

Bill drained the scorching tea and put the cup down on the hearth. Standing up, he wrapped his arms around her.

"They'll come after you, you know."

He smelt of fish and sweat. Of a husband under the soil and a lover under the tide.

"I know."

⌢

That night she went under the sea for one last time. They still clung to the cable, eating nothing but ones and zeroes. Ragged fur stretched over ribs. She swam between them. None paid her any attention, their skin buckled with limpets grinding in sores.

This time she spotted him, his brindled fur moulting with each brush of water. She tried to catch his gaze. Swim so she could stare into his eyes. The cable blocked her. In desperation, she grasped his waist. Tried to haul him away from his addiction. With a lazy twitch he flicked her loose, sending her tumbling across the seabed, silt and dead scales rising around her.

⌢

The hut was brick built, double skinned and barely bigger than her shed. Triple locks bolted across the metal door. She soon wrenched those free, not caring if hidden cameras transmitted her vandalism back to some control room in a landlocked city.

She worked quickly, placing the satchel underneath the vast cable, wedged against the concrete floor. Trailing the detonating cord, she walked backwards out of the door, and sat in the long grass. She sat for a long time. Watched the tide wrap in upon itself. Then, when it started to turn, she switched the detonator.

The hut unfurled. Splinters of fibre-optic sleeted through the air. Bricks pushed outwards. Several chips cut her skin to ribbons and she ran her fingers along the wounds, sucking her fingers to taste the truth of the sea in her blood.

The waves bubbled and the first seals broke the surface, jaws open, eyes closed and spines to the sea. They did not dive or grasp for the beach. Instead the tide rucked their lifeless bodies back and forth. From the cliffs, she could not gauge which ones wore different souls under their skin. Could not see if one of them wore brindled fur. Her eyesight was tired. She was tired.

The vehicle sirens sounded like a flock of geese in full voice, until they parked behind her. Margaret's hand went down to the second satchel tucked under her legs, her fingers playing with the thin cable coming out of the corner. They would lock her away from the coast. Box her in granite far from the sea. She knew that. Maybe she deserved it. On the beach the waves tipped one corpse after another onto the sand. She would always have the salted water in her blood.

Letting the bag strap go, she stood, raised her hands and put them behind her head.

ABYSSAL

by Lorraine Schein

Epipelagic (sunlight/photic): **From the surface to 660 feet down. The illuminated zone at the surface of the sea where enough sunlight is available for photosynthesis.**

The sun sank below the horizon, a bright coral reef that cast spines of wavering red light on the gray water.

Will I ever see the sun again? Katexa thought as she lowered herself into the Bathystar's left arm and closed the hatch. She hoped this was the way to save her stubborn family.

She had argued with them before she left.

"Katexa," her mother had said. "We know the sea is rising again. But our clan vowed not to abandon the land—you know this. We stay human, as long as we stay above."

Her family was among the last humans to defy the ocean's relentless advance, and now even the small island they lived on was being eroded.

There was still one hope, Katexa knew, blasphemous as it was— she had read the archives and knew of the emigrants. They could migrate to the ocean's depths too, if the Bathystar still worked well enough.

The archives were clear: Though the oceans had become filled with dead zones where no fish or sea life survived, and the melting of the polar ice caps had flooded homes on land so many times, a contingent of dissenters had set off to establish a separatist colony in the sea's depths. No further record of them remained, only stories.

Their only option might be to descend. Which is why she had to go first—to prove to her family there was another way.

Mesopelagic (twilight) from 660 ft. down to 3,300 ft. The name for this zone stems from the Greek; meson, meaning middle. Although some light penetrates this second layer, it is insufficient for photosynthesis. At about 500 m the water also becomes depleted of oxygen. Organisms survive this environment by having efficient gills or minimizing movement. Many organisms that live here are bioluminescent.

Katexa had heard those stories many times: How humans first descended after the Great Floods that came to cover most of the Earth, going down in heavy individual submarines shaped like coffins, cushioned submarines that could be lived in, built to withstand the enormous pressure of life at the bottom of the sea.

Less than two percent of the ocean floor had been explored before then, but necessity drove the desperate deeper. Tired of the hardships of life on dwindling land and the constant floods, some had decided to stay in the depths, becoming Abyssals—those living in the Abyssal zone, the deepest part of the sea. Through bioengineering and adaptation, they evolved into deep sea creatures.

Her grandmother had told Katexa that even one of their own ancestors had become Abyssal. But her mother and father would say nothing on the subject.

The Bathystars now sat mostly idle. These were plankotech versions of the ancient Bathysphere (from the Greek: *bathus*, "deep" and *sphaira*, "sphere"), an air-filled submersible ball lowered into the ocean on a cable.

The Bathystar was also spherical, its center built to resist enormous pressure. It had five protrusions, like the arms of a five-pointed star that rotated it through the water slowly but efficiently. There were window-like gills in these arms, and each one was a room.

Katexa was the only one who still piloted them, for short trips between islands.

Katexa had kissed her mother and hugged her sister goodbye. She had prepared for her descent for months, wearing a face mask that shut out most of the light, and never going out during the day, avoiding the sun.

The Bathystar floated, dipping below her. She climbed into the hatch of the top star-arm, and it hissed shut above her. She hoisted herself into the steering seat and found the controls.

She set the course for down, further down than she'd ever gone.

Abyssopelagic (lower midnight): Abyssal zone from 13,000 ft. down to above the ocean floor. The name is derived from Greek (ábyssos), meaning "bottomless" (from the time when the deep ocean, or abyss, was believed to be bottomless). Very few creatures live in the cold temperatures, high pressures and complete darkness of this depth.

At first the waters were almost totally dark, only lit by the top lights of the Bathystar. Then Katexa saw a school of lantern fish, bodies glowing gently, swimming up to the surface in search of food. Since they only fed at night, she didn't have to look at her diurnalband to know that meant it must be night above-world. Next a baitball of flashlight fish passed by, the lights under their eyes blinking in a glowing green Morse code, and luminous plankton that looked like little stars. She put on a head lantern until her eyes soon got used to dark.

Her bed was in the second arm of the Bathystar; a small kitchen with a cabinet stocked with condensed nonperishables and a tank for purifying the water from outside were in the third. It was hard to tell how much time had passed. Fading at last, Katexa climbed into bed and fell asleep.

When she awoke, she made her way back to the control room in the Bathystar's clear arm, saw it and gasped.

The Transparensea bobbed above her outside, glowing, a transparent floating ghost—its abdominal skin so thin she could see its heart, liver and intestines. It was a radiant green, because it had just been eating a meal of marine ferns and sea caterpillars.

Katexa had descended deeper, deeper than anyone from her clan ever had before, and this was her reward.

The creature's head tilted toward her as she steered past it. Its skull was translucent, but she could still see the outline of a blue whorled brain, crossed by faint sparking synapses. The Transparensea looked like her sister in profile, but then it turned and she saw it had no eyes—just luminous oval hollows where they should be.

She stammered out a greeting into the microphone, but though it halted and seemed to listen, it soon floated away.

Maybe they no longer understand human speech, as we have not yet learned theirs of ripples and dark light, she thought. One day her descendants might forget land speech too. Katexa wondered if people would be happier then. She smiled, imagining her family communicating this way.

Could this be the ancestor her grandmother had told her stories of? Then maybe in time and with genetic engineering, her family could become a new generation of Abyssals, look like them. She had heard them described as ugly, but she thought the creature eerily beautiful.

Hadopelagic: Hadal zone. Waters below 20,000 ft. The deep water in ocean trenches. The name is derived from the realm of Hades, the underworld in Greek mythology. This zone is mostly unknown, and very few species are known to live here. However, many organisms live in hydrothermal vents. The abyssal plain is covered with soft sludge composed of dead organisms from above.

Creatures become more than eyeless here. They are formless, eat sludge and sleep under eons of decayed dead. They crawl and breathe in the crevices of time.

Katexa wrote in the Bathystar's log: *I miss land and trees with roots. And natural light. In the dark sea that surrounds me, I long for the sun. And earth, before the waters came.*

The Transparensea hovered over the Bathystar, pressed its sinuous face against the clear curvature of the bed-arm as she slept.

One day we will rise again, grow fins, then legs. The words flowed, bubbled into the space between her mind and its floating.

It has been said that more is known about the Moon than the deepest parts of the ocean.

BIOLUMINESCENCE

by Maria Haskins

The boy is sleeping. For a moment she stands in the door just looking at him, at the unfamiliar size and shape of his body beneath the covers.

Her hair and footsteps are wet from outside. Water drips on the carpet, soaking into the floor beneath.

I've been away too long.

She almost turns to go without waking him. Almost.

She lifts him up and carries him out of the house, across the road, to the ocean. It's farther than she remembers, and he is heavier, his legs much longer than when she carried him last time, but he does not wake until she lays him down on the dock.

Fear flickers across his face when he sees her leaning over him.

"Mom?"

The word slips into her, beneath her skin, takes hold.

"Thomas."

Around them, the grey ocean heaves and breathes. She can feel its pull, its pulse and rhythm inside veins and marrow. Sitting down, she slips her bare feet into the dark water, a shimmer of bioluminescent plankton tracing her movements.

Closing her eyes, she sees the continental shelf sloping out from the shoreline, the submerged mountains and plains of the ocean floor beyond. The dock is clinging to a precipice; her toes dangle over the abyss.

Opening her eyes, she sees the shadows of the things that were and are: beach and pines, house. Faraway lights in windows. Distant stars above.

"We used to sit here. You and me. Watching stars."

He nods.

Neither of them looks up at the sky.

Somewhere straight out from the dock, beyond the horizon she cannot see, is the place where she descended. She remembers zipping into her thermo-suit, stepping into the elevator pod, into the familiar buzz and jostle of co-workers, leaving the choppy grey of the northwest Pacific's surface behind. Descending. Through the epipelagic sunlight zone, through the mesopelagic twilight zone, through the bathypelagic midnight zone. Then, the mining station: a sprawling artefact of metal and glass, narrow beams of light revealing groups of robots, crawling like crabs over fissures and vents and sediment; mining, digging, cutting, drilling, ever deeper.

Endeavour Ridge. Black smokers. Hydrothermal vents. Fault line. Cobalt. Nickel. Copper. Six thousand five hundred feet. Two thousand metres. Give or take.

These numbers, these words, these names and places: she turns them over in her mind like smooth rocks left in the pocket of an old jacket, found again.

"Does dad know you're back?"

"No."

Thomas turns away. He is tall and angular. Dark haired, dark eyed. Changed.

Like me.

"He never wanted you to go. Neither did I."

"You were just a baby when I left."

The small child pulling at her pant-leg at the door, looking up. Pleading.

"Not a baby. I was five. I remember it."

She's lost for a moment.

"How old are you now?"

He gives her a long look.

"Twelve."

She moves her feet in the water: tide and current tug and whisper against her skin. Below is the heavy darkness rolling over the wrecks and ruins of the past.

"Why did you leave?" he asks.

"I wanted to go. More than anything else."

It's not what he wants to hear, but it's the truth. Yet, how can he understand? He hasn't descended and ascended through the darkness lit only by creatures illuminated from within. He hasn't twisted in the heated currents above the magma glow, or felt the gentle touch of the deep-sea jellies' tentacles. He hasn't seen the sparks of blue-green fire come to life around him in the dark.

"You should have stayed with me."

She says nothing. Thomas is quiet for a long time. Maybe he's crying. She looks at him but does not touch, remembering the fear passing across his face when he first saw her.

Seven years. Has it been that long?

"What's it like down there?" His voice is small and brittle.

When she answers, her words are only surface: calm, still, opaque. Not the dizzying abyss of memories beneath.

"It's cold. Dark. But there is heat and light, too. It's beautiful."

In the water, bioluminescent sparks gather around her hands and fingers: clinging, holding on, letting go.

"You promised me you would come back."

His voice is harder now.

"I came back."

She moves her feet in the dark water, admiring the shimmer ignited by her movement and her skin.

"Mom. How did you get here?"

She doesn't like his tone. It is so sharp that it makes her shiver and crack.

"I swam."

Descending and ascending. Through the layers, through the darkness, through the light. That word, calling her back:

"Mom."

"Thomas…"

He interrupts her.

"You drowned, mom. Dad told me. When the quake hit. Everything at Endeavour Ridge… The fault line…"

He sobs. Her thoughts blur and twist. She feels her face slip, but manages to hold on to it a little longer.

"Water got in. We were all drowning."

She doesn't tell him about the light. She doesn't tell him about the light igniting all around her, a million tiny points of blue-green fire moving as one, its amorphous shape shifting and rippling, touching her, flickering across her skin, entering her mouth and nose, eyes and pores. She doesn't tell him about lungs and heart and skull and mind splitting apart in an instant of despair and terror, and then: relief, calm, light. Being. Something else.

"Why didn't you come back? You said you would."

"Thomas."

"You promised me."

She looks down at her naked body, sees the shimmering cracks and veins breaking through the skin, through the surface. Yet even now, it's hard to slip this skin, harder than it should be. Because he wants to see her. Because he wants everything to be the way it was. Because even now, he wants her to stay.

"I can't," she says.

"You promised."

There is no mercy in his words. Nothing to hold onto.

Her face slips, limbs too, the pull of the water is too strong: the ocean beneath pulsing with the light spilling through the fractures in her skin.

"Thomas."

But not even saying his name out loud can hold her together anymore.

She glides into the water. Eyes and hair dissolve, sinews and joints give way, all she is and was, is turned back to blue-green glow.

"Mom!"

A million points of light and memory gather and move as one—shimmering, ascending, descending—as the trail of bioluminescence slips away from him into the deep beneath.

PORTRAIT OF MY WIFE AS A BOAT

by Samantha Murray

She comes home later and later even though the nights are starting earlier than they were.

I feel cross and wronged, and pretend not to see her as she hesitates briefly on the doorstep. I bow my head to my stitching. A new quilt, this one—with gold, russet and red, colors for the Fall that is coming.

I do not look at her directly but I notice that her hair is stiff with salt and spray. She is barefoot and leaves little curved dark marks on the floorboards as she crosses. I cave and tell her, "There is rice on the stove."

"I am not hungry," she says, and her voice creaks like old, old wood. "I am tired, I'm going to bed." She rests her hand for a moment on my shoulder, but lightly, so lightly.

That night she tosses and writhes like she is caught on the tides. The bed-sheets are twisted asunder and I wake and sit up in bed. I touch her arm and whisper soothingly but she will not be soothed.

⌢

She smells of linseed, of citrus, the oil that she rubs into all of the little tiny cracks in her face. When she leaves she kisses me and I taste the sea.

⌢

Then comes two days and two wild, gusty nights she is gone. Most of my stitching I have to unpick again and again. When she comes in I swell up to her. "Where have you been?" I cry, and my voice rises high and wails at her like a spiteful wind, "Where have you been?"

She opens her mouth but she does not seem to have any words left. She holds her palms out towards me, and stands there, squelching.

She looks both harder and smoother, and deeper brown. I can see that she has come back just for me. I can see too that four walls are four too many, and that the hooked rug and the narrow bed heaped with pillows just make her obscurely miserable. She has come back for me, and I am not the sea.

⌒

The next time she leaves I sit with my stitching and stare at it. Then I put it down. I follow her across the old reserve where you can smell the big, old peppermint trees, down over the dune and across the sand. The sun has baked the sand hot and I feel the heat under my feet but I do not hasten my steps. Some things are meant to hurt.

She stands at the shoreline, and I see she is already curving, curving, stretching, turning, curving. Till she lies, half in the water, rocking.

She is the shape of two open cupped hands pressed together. The shape of a coracle, in welsh *cwrwgl*, the light little boats from the place I was born. She has a mast though, as they did not, standing proud against the sky. Her hull is heartwood with swirling shades of grey, like ilmenite in wet sand. She is a thing of beauty, but that doesn't surprise me at all because I knew that already, I knew that always.

I lift my leg over the side of her. There is room, just for one. She rocks back and forth, and her sail unfurls and billows out. I think she is pleased.

Her rocking motion edges us forward off the sand-bank and into the deeper water. Light and delicate she whips along towards the white-tipped waves. I do not speak to her again but I run my fingers over the sun-warmed wood of her gunwale. What are words but an anchor that drags behind her, slowing her down, making her stop, binding her to the land. You don't say 'I love you' to a boat, you don't, you don't.

⌒

The wind has picked up and is blowing my hair back from my face. She will take me to shore now, I know. I will stand on the sand and watch her as she heads out towards the sun that is drowning itself at the horizon. I will go back to my hearth and sit and wait although I know she will not come. I will start a new quilt, one for winter this time. One with pelagic hues—cerulean and cyan, with flecks at the edges white as the tips of the waves.

SILVERMOUTH

by Doug Murano

1.

See young Shelley Bachman—hair like cornsilk trailing in the breeze behind her, summer dress fluttering, barefoot. She's walking on tiptoes across Lake Ophelia, arms out like a scarecrow, tracing a line under the full moon along a railroad trestle that spans high above the lake. Hear her humming a folk tune, murmuring the lyrics she only half remembers. The words lift high into the clear August sky above and fall to the calm surface of the lake fifty feet below.

Shelley has brought a ring and a song and a wish. She has come for Silvermouth.

2.

Big as a Shetland pony with eyes like tea-saucers, they call the creature Silvermouth on account of the hundreds of steel hooks trailing fishing line buried in jaws so powerful they could snap a man's femur. The fish (who wouldn't earn its name until many years after it was first sighted) showed up in Norah's history nearly a hundred years ago, around the time the railroad trestle went up across the lake that formed the town's eastern edge.

They say, during the trestle's construction, one of the workers (Thumbs Sinclair, whose family still lives in Norah, carrying that shame all these years later) dropped a hammer into the water and woke it up. Trouble followed—support beams trembling or outright cracking from an unseen impact below, odd shifts in the lakebed making it impossible to drill true.

If you believe the stories passed down as old men and their grandsons tossed baited lines into Lake Ophelia and dreamed of tying into something monstrous, Silvermouth's handiwork added a full season onto construction. Graham Brown, who towered over the other workers at nearly seven feet tall, disappeared into the water without a trace during that horrible month of August.

For a time, the railroad trestle fed lines of boxcars into the town from the Big Cities beyond, an artery laid down across the prairie which carried in everything Norah needed to grow from a tiny dot on the flat, treeless plain into something more prosperous.

And with every snapped line, Silvermouth's legend grew.

3.

Let's get back to Shelley, who knows a thing or two about fish stories. Rumors of sweaty dalliances in haylofts. Tales of illicit coupling after barn dances. Of ale and cider and cinnamon summer and hands and thighs and lips and eyes that promise all. Shelley could recite so many stories, and as it often goes in the small, out-of-the-way potholes of civilization the world over, she has lived almost none of them. And what of it, either way? Even so, every disapproving stare buries a hook in her. The cost deepens with each passing season.

She has come without rod, without hook, without bait to call Silvermouth's name in the moonlight.

And so she does. She takes a golden band from her ring finger, tosses it into the lake and, peering into the water below, calls for the beast.

To her amazement, the creature answers.

Shelly watches a circular ripple appear on Lake Ophelia, as a stone makes when thrown into calm water. Then, a halo of gossamer threads breaches the surface as Silvermouth's cavernous, puckering mouth and vast head rise up into the night. Moonlight fills its saucer eyes, and they shine out like lanterns. Even from her perch high up on the trestle Shelley can't quite still the quake in her every cell or the vertigo that has toppled her sense of balance. Like every man, woman and child who grew up in Norah, she has heard the tales. She adjusts her feet and finds steady footing again.

The creature regards her quietly and nods as if giving her leave to speak her piece. The hooks in its maw jingle like pocket change.

"I wanted to see something everyone wants but nobody gets to have," says Shelley. "I want it more than anything."

Without warning, Silvermouth slips back under. Shelley waits, cries the great fish's name, nearly leaves when the gigantic creature's body breaches the surface. It rises into the silvery night sky, twirling, sending pinwheels of lake water in every direction, its monofilament beard a dazzling starburst. With a thundering splash, it returns to the water. Once more, its head rises to greet Shelley, and it once again nods in encouragement, in expectation.

In spite of the awe bordering on terror churning through her chest, Shelley bends her knees in a curtsey and bounds upward in a pirouette.

The great fish mirrors Shelley with a spin of its own and begins to swim across Lake Ophelia, dorsal fin cutting the water and leaving great wakes to either side. Shelley gives chase down the trestle and when Silvermouth breaches into the misty air once more Shelley leaps in response. She forgets her terror. Moonlight reflects against the ripping water and back up at Shelley, casting dancing shadows like great fish scales upon her milky skin.

She twirls, watching the shimmering scales tattoo their pattern across her skin. She dances. She runs the length of the trestle and back again, following the path the great beast cuts across the lake. She cries out in delight at every leap.

Then, the creature flips once more into the air, splashes down into the lake and disappears.

Gasping for breath, Shelley falls to her knees and calls for Silvermouth. She waits, but there is no answer. She calls again and again, and the only answer is the hum of clouds of mosquitoes. Holding tight to the rail, she leans out over Lake Ophelia, forgetting the stories. She has barely enough time to get a glimpse of the fish's fin cutting a path toward the nearest support beam before the trestle shudders mightily.

Something snaps like fishing line. Shelley tumbles out into the moonlight and falls as shadows of scales dance across her skin.

4.

The sun rises over Lake Ophelia, covering the shattered trestle's beams in pink light.

Somewhere along the western bank, two hands emerge from the dark water and grab fistfuls of marsh grass. Elbows and knees dig deep into the muck as a female figure slides up out of the water and collapses. There, she lies panting ensconced within the greenery. Her dripping hair is the color of cornsilk and gossamer line. Silver threads form a neat trail in the water nearby. Pushing herself to her knees, she spits out the last hook. She rises to her feet and takes her first shaky steps away from town.

A FISH FOR OPHELIA

by Craig Wallwork

Ophelia was ten years old the day she drowned her father. She ran to the old water pump, filled two buckets and carried them back to their caravan. Inside her father lay on a patchwork quilt, his hands balled as if rapping on death's door. Red jacquard curtains suffocated sunlight and his eyes seemed to endlessly survey the ceiling for an angel wing, or the Devil's hand. Ophelia couldn't tell which. She placed the two buckets on the floor and knelt beside him. With breath scented by Parma Violets, she said softly, "I know how to save you, Pa." Propping him up on pillows, she added, "I found you a cure."

The only other witness to this act of mercy was Gill, a lonely bronzed goldfish. For fifteen years, Gill's home had been a glass bowl perched upon a nesting table in the caravan. An unlikely apostle, Gill had followed the life of Ophelia's father with hushed reverence and marvel. It had seen him abandon his role as a sideshow's Ballyhoo once emphysema cheated him of fortissimo. It saw him coughing and crying in equal measure due to his illness and seclusion. It also saw him convulse the day Gerty arrived. Ophelia's father had one sister, which to him was one more than he needed. Like her brother, Gerty had spent most of her life travelling in sideshows, and so was accustomed to never settling anyplace for too long. It came as no surprise then when she turned up at his door one morning carrying a suitcase in her hand and baby in her stomach.

"The father?" he asked, indifferently.

"A local gazoonie," she replied, stacking a drawer with her clothes.

"He around much?"

"Stayed long enough to wipe his dick dry before jumping the next boxcar out of town, if that's what you mean?"

That was all that was said on the matter. For all her naivety concerning love, it was Gerty who looked after her brother when his lungs began to fail, and in return, he watched her swell like a balloon before pushing out a baby nine months later into a room no bigger than a shoebox. The screaming of a baby hankering for love and nourishment proved too much for Gerty. She would go for long walks into town and not return until after dark, leaving her brother the task of looking after the child. One day, she went out and never returned. The baby was his, and he called her Ophelia.

⌢

Ophelia placed a large plastic sack over her father's head, pulled back the bed sheet exposing gangly legs the colour of church candles, and rolled down the remaining length, creating a lucent pupa that held him whole. A fog of breath upon the plastic blurred his mouth. His eyes remained fixed upon the ceiling. When Ophelia came into view, she smiled and whispered, "Ain't nothing to worry about, Pa." Water sloshed and spilled in generous measure as Ophelia brought the buckets to the bedside.

"I'll do the same as I do with Gill," she said.

It had been Ophelia's job to look after Gill. Since she was five years old, she would corral that fish into a small mason jar filled with water before taking his bowl to the water pump to wash the inside free of algae. When the bowl shone like a glacier, she filled it again to the lip with fresh cold water. Her father would inspect the work as if appraising a diamond. "Good," he would say peering into the bowl. "Now, what did I tell you?" he asked.

Ophelia would reply immediately, "If a goldfish is happy and clean, it'll live forever."

She never forgot that.

Ophelia emptied the first bucket into the plastic sack, immersing her father's face in cold water. He gasped, releasing from his mouth tiny bubbles the shape of miniscule jellyfish. She poured the other bucket in and he thrashed as the plastic pupa filled. Ophelia ran out into the cold September light and filled them again. On her return, she found him still, mouth agape and eyes wide open as if resting under a calm river. She poured more water in and kept doing so until he was completely submerged. With the remaining twine, she tied the ends of the plastic together and left him to drown upon the bed.

The following day, Ophelia cleaned the caravan and harvested food for the winter. The next she read and drank nettle tea. Occasionally she checked her father to see how he was doing. On the third day, she saw his skin turn from alabaster to a pale golden colour. On the fifth, deep gashes appeared between the fingers of his ribs. By the time windows frosted with ice, and strong winds toured the landscape of her hometown, her father had shrunk to half his size. Christmas came and the bones of his arm splintered and widened. It wasn't long after this his legs fused together, and yellowy legions swelled in patches all over his body. Alopecia followed in the New Year, as did atrophy of his eyelids. Then finally, on the morning of January 18th, Ophelia's father took his first breath again. Careful not to spill the water, Ophelia untied the twine from one end of the plastic before reaching inside. He was small enough now to fit in her hand. His golden tail beat against her palm. His mouth opened and closed as if singing a silent opera. She held him carefully, her warm breath calming him.

"You're better now," she said.

She carried him gently to the fishbowl and lowered him in. For the rest of the day she watched her father and Gill swim together for the first time with the understanding that in giving her father a second chance at life, Ophelia had also given Gill a life without loneliness.

GREEN

by Sharon Jimenez

A peacock's harsh, cawing cry silences everything else in their Floridian neighborhood, and then the screaming of the unseen cicadas returns in full force. It's not yet dark enough to be dusk, although the sun's going in that direction soon enough. The girls return to their task, plucking snails from their mother's red cabbages and sticking them, with great concentration, onto each other's bare arms. They've never seen the peacocks, but legends abound of a local rich man's private zoo, released into the wilds of their neighborhood when his fortunes failed. Their parents and neighbors tell that story every time they hear the cry echoing off the bleached white concrete of their driveways and the walls of their cinderblock homes.

The girls do not need to see the peacocks to know their cries, after a childhood of hearing this story. They are more interested in their garden's snails.

The snails have names. The girls babble to one another, sometimes—words their parents and uncles and neighbors don't understand, and chirruping nonsense passed back and forth like birdsong, and hushed, matter-of-fact proclamations when they are alone together. More often than not, though, they are in silent agreement of the facts.

The sun is behind the tops of the trees and the evening clouds, and the ambient light is tolerable—not too hot, not too bright, the harsh yellows cut to softer, dappled greens by the wild growth of the backyard garden.

The girl on the left shows a reddish-orange snail to the girl on the right; she points at a spot on her forearm, near the crook of her elbow.

The other girl carefully sets the snail in place on her sister's arm. They catalogue this snail's name and placement for later, then go back to searching the cabbage for his fellows.

There is a bucket where the snails are supposed to go, according to their mother and father. They don't like the thought of the snails being in the bucket, but some of them—the ones that seem a bit naughty, the ones that are too big to stay stuck onto their skin—end up in the bucket anyway.

There is a rustle in the springy yucca and bamboo stalks that line the fence between their yard and their neighbor's; the girls do not look. They've met their neighbors, and they can be nice enough—nice, but loud. The rustling continues, disrupting their shared silence and mixing unpleasantly with the screaming of the cicadas. It's still something to ignore—the neighborhood cat always meows loudly at them, so they know it's not him, and therefore it's not something that needs them.

There is another shrieking peacock's call, this time from just inside the bamboo, and the girls raise their heads—it's closer and louder than they've ever heard it before, and they've never seen a peacock in person, only photos and drawings. The girl on the left is more excited than her sister is at the prospect of seeing a real, live peacock. The girl on the right is merely excited to see her sister happy.

The thick green stalks part—

—it is a man with skin like crushed velvet, his hands resting on the bamboo, his feet bare in the dark silver soil. The light coming in through the leaves makes his skin a lighter green in the places where it isn't gleaming emerald. His eyes flicker between the girls, his head tilted to one side, and they look back down at the cabbages and their snails.

His bare toes grasp and clench into the soft, cool soil; the girls clench and grasp their own bare toes into the dirt. The girl on the right gently plucks a snail from the underside of one of their mother's cabbages, putting it into the bucket. He crouches down and gives the cabbage a poke, mimicking them, but he still towers over their heads.

The peacock cries again; both girls look up, watching the man's throat work as he opens his mouth and utters the noise. It bounces off the walls of their house behind them, filling up what's visible of the cloudy, graying sky. The sisters regard him for a moment or two, carefully assessing the situation. The call ends and he gives them a sharp, brittle grin. The silence stands still for a moment, before a dog a few houses away starts barking and the cicadas hidden in the trees around them resume their nightly screaming.

The girl on the left gathers up the snails on her arms and puts them in her sister's hands. The girl on the right puts the snails into the bucket and then holds the bucket out to the man, impressed with his talent. He takes the bucket, gingerly twisting it this way and that, his eyes wide with interest, his nostrils flaring happily.

The girl on the right finds a snail in the grass and hands it to her sister, who holds it proudly up to the man's face. His mouth darts forward with a swift bobbing motion, his teeth brushing her fingertips. There is a sharp crunch, and his eyes—gold, they decide before looking away, like the rings their parents wear on their fingers—light up. He reaches into the bucket and shoves a handful into his mouth like popcorn, little bits of shell and snail slime sticking to his chin.

It takes him a couple of minutes to empty the bucket, as they watch in fascinated silence. He licks his lips and the ends of his fingers, thumping the plastic bucket onto the dirt. The girls look at the empty bucket—all those snails gone, all those names eaten—and back up at the man. He regards them for a moment, before opening his fist over the empty bucket. Feathers fall out in a tidy pile—jewel-green and brilliant paint-blue, iridescent and flat. He holds out his other fist and opens it more carefully, showing them a pair of long, sparse feathers, shining and green with the big, shimmering peacock-eye on the ends.

It is a good trade, all things considered. The girls look up from their new treasures, but the man is gone. At the far end of the street, a peacock cries out, silencing the cicadas.

COLD BURN

by Shannon Connor Winward

The marsh was a cold, dark place. Most nights, the wisp could only lie in the muck, the essence of itself spread far across the shallows. But sometimes, when boredom began to itch and loneliness creep, the wisp could draw itself together and rise above its watery bed, buoyed by the marsh's foul breath—that magic miasma of life and rot. If the wisp wanted it enough, and if it waited long enough in between, it could incite itself to burn as bright as headlights, as bright as the moon.

But like those ephemeral lights, the wisp burned cold. It was left always with a hunger for warmth—the kind only the living have to offer.

Normally, the wisp preferred fellas. It especially liked young ones, the wild ones, loud and reckless and hot-blooded—the kind that drove with the top down even in winter. It liked their red cheeks and ale-bright eyes, the drunker the better. The wisp had no interest in old ladies, ordinarily.

But there was something about this biddy that roused the wisp from slumber. At her age, at this dark hour, she had no business on a road like Smuggler's Run—the twisty stretch of ramshackle bridges and mud connecting the docks and bars to the turnpike. But she marched along like she knew just where she was going, like she had a mighty purpose. With her long black shawl trailing behind, her walking stick clutched to her bosom like a scepter, and her chin held high, the old lady looked like she was asking to be taken. So, the wisp decided to oblige.

With a twist and a tug and a shimmy, the wisp pulled itself up from the cold mud and let its beacon shine.

The old lady saw, for sure. She paused, her breath coming in quick startled puffs, her face turned out from the road toward where the wisp had coalesced. It felt the heat of her gaze—oh, yes. It made the wisp feel giddy—it skipped and spun, thinking *come, come. Feed me, make me warm.*

But the old lady did not come.

The wisp flitted closer. Sometimes, it wasn't enough to be the dancing light, urging them into the dark like moths to flame. Sometimes, it had to put on a show to get fellas to slow their cars, pull over, step off the road. The shape of a leg here, the narrowness of a waist there, the hint of a pretty face—it took more out of the wisp, burned it up quicker, but it got them going.

But the old bag? What did old ladies like?

The wisp thought hard, harder than it had in a long time. Finally, with a trill of triumph, it unraveled two pointy ears, a slinky middle, a tail. *Purr, purr,* called the wisp. *I'm lost, come feed me. Make me warm.*

The old lady bent with effort to squint into the dark. She waggled her old lady fingers and said, "Come now," but still, she herself would not budge.

This troubled the wisp. It hurt to take form, it hurt to think, and it was cold—oh, so cold. The old woman's life burned like an oven with good scents wafting from it. Hungry, shivering, the wisp came closer.

Then: *aah*, thought the wisp. Its tail grew longer, its body thicker, shaggier with remembered shape—a big red dog, the kind that would sleep curled at your feet by the hearth. *Woof*, cried the wisp. *I'm a dog. I'm lost. Come make me warm.*

Something changed in the old woman's face. The bag she carried slipped from her shoulder and landed on the road with a *thunk*. "Lady?" she croaked, and the wisp felt whorls of satisfaction. It was working, it was working—but, no. The old woman still would not leave the road.

"Come on," she intoned, urging the wisp. "Come on, girl."

The wisp slipped closer. What was it going to take?

Hovering, shuddering, near the edge of Smuggler's Run, the wisp caught a whiff of perfume. *Lavender*, it thought, not knowing how it knew the name of such a thing. The wisp imagined long arms and tender wrists, dabbled with scent. Also ears, neck, bosom. *Well*, thought the wisp, and with a flap and a flutter it grew arms and wrists and ears and all of those things, until it stood by the road in the shape of a girl.

Seeing this, the old lady made a mournful sound. She took a shaky step forward and put out a hand, as if longing to touch. *Aha!* the wisp thought, dancing back. *Whatever works. Come!*

But the old woman jabbed her walking stick into the wet shoulder of the road, and would go no farther. The wisp quivered and glowed with rage. *I'm so cold!* it shouted. *Why won't you come?!?*

"Enough!" the old lady hollered back. She jabbed her stick and stomped her foot and pointed at the ground. "You come here now, or so help me God..."

To the wisp's great surprise, it slunk forward and bowed its head beneath the old lady's wrath. *Witch!* the wisp thought, grumbling and morose, but unable to resist.

"How many boys have you taken from this road?" the old woman demanded. *A lot.* "How many more poor mothers' hearts must break?"

The wisp did not want to hear this. The wisp wanted nothing of mothers, of grief. The wisp only wanted to be *warm*, to be *full*, to stop the empty places inside from gaping, shaking, needing so very much. But the damn crone went on, reciting the names of dead fellas that the wisp had lured away—*Michael, Edward, Jimmy, John, Eugene, Stanley, Walter, Ike*—hot-blooded and wild, each one a gutted flame in the wisp's belly, never enough.

Too late, the wisp realized what the old lady was about: the names were a charm, drawing the wisp ever closer, binding it, forcing it to remember.

Theodore, the lady said, and the wisp saw clear, then: the red-faced, bright-eyed boy, thundering down Smuggler's Run in his shiny motorcar, and she, the wisp, right there beside him, the wind whipping her hair, stealing her breath. It was winter, and cold, so cold, the road covered with ice, but Teddy was a damned fool. Before long the world flipped upside down and the wisp was in the mud, the moon and stars burning cold fire in her dying eyes. At the last, the wisp thought of her mama, waiting, waiting at home by the hearth for a girl who would never return.

"Hah," said the old woman, bringing her hand down quick. Snapped from its reverie, the wisp tried to fly away but instead smacked into an invisible wall. The wisp looked up, saw the moon, encircled for a moment, then eclipsed as the lid of a mason jar slid in place.

The wisp panicked, zipping this where and that, but could not escape. Pressing against the glass, the wisp found itself staring into the old woman's milky eye.

"All right, Agnes Jean, you settle down now."

But the marsh, the wisp thought. *The gaseous breath, the magic—* without it, the wisp knew, it would soon dissipate, be gone for good. But as the old woman nestled the jar against her chest, the wisp found itself curling eagerly, sleepily against the glass, soaking up the delicious heat there—the kind that never burned out. The wisp's body pulsed with flickering peace, enough to light the way as the old woman began her long trek home.

DOWN BY THE WEEPING SHORE

by Natalia Theodoridou

The orphanage is perched on a hill overlooking the lake. My room is plain, almost spartan, but it suits me well enough. I have a desk by the window, a dresser, a bed. That's all I ever needed. Two months here and the other teachers have already started teasing me about how little I own: no pictures, no souvenirs, no special box full of letters. Like a woman without a past, they say. Nothing to hold her back. Nothing to tie her down.

I do my hair up and glance out the window before I join the rest of them to prepare for tonight. The day is unremarkable enough—if I were not from around here, I could well think it to be like any other day of the year.

I take in the view for a moment. The lake is still, the shore empty.

⌒

"We used to lose a child every year before we dreamt up the paper swan trick," the headmistress tells me as she shapes the paper mâché into feathers and glues them onto the main body of the bird. "It was the children who first came up with the idea and asked us to try it. Before that, the swan would start singing in the middle of the night and one child..." She trails off as she focuses on a particularly tricky bit of plumage. "One child would just get up and amble down to the lake, as if under a spell." She pauses. "We stood guard, but they always managed to sneak out. They'd be in the water before we even realized

-146-

one was missing." A sigh. "We came close to shutting the orphanage down, but then where would all these children go? Besides, there will always be children in the area, orphan or not." She shakes her head, then raises her eyes to glance at me briefly. "You're lucky, dear. That was all before your time," she says.

She's wrong, of course. I know the story well. It goes something like this:

Once upon a time, this land was ruled by a prince who was kind and young, who loved birds and poetry, and whose childhood friend and companion drowned one night in the lake—this lake, this very one. The prince sat by the water and mourned, inconsolable, for weeks, until a passing god took pity on him. The god turned the prince into a swan so that grief would no longer weigh him down, just as water does not wet the feathers of a swan. But the prince's sorrow was so great that, once a year, on the day his friend drowned, the swan sang his loss until a child was lured into the water and perished.

They always found the children a week later, their cold bodies perfectly preserved, their skin smelling faintly of water lilies and moss, a single white feather caught in their hair. The peasants hunted down the swan and butchered it, and killed all the other swans in the area for good measure, but the next year the lone swan was there again, floating gracefully by the lake bank, singing its doleful song.

We whispered this story to one another every night when I lived here first—an orphan, back then, and look at me now, a teacher myself. We shared it like a prayer, hoping that would stop it from happening again and again and again. With our childish minds, we hated the winged prince as much as we felt sorry for him.

I remember the swan's song piercing the night. I remember cowering under the blankets as Marie slipped out of bed and walked barefoot out of the dorm. And I remember my friend's body, found a week later to the day, covered in a blanket by the lake, a cold, lifeless arm poking out. I wondered if they would find a white feather tucked in her hair. I never asked whether they did.

"Here, help me with this," the headmistress says, pointing at the paper swan's long, thin neck.

I hold it upright while she covers its base with real down.

"So, this works?" I ask, not yet daring to believe it.

"It has, so far," she says. "Let's hope it works again tonight."

It's the only time of the year the children are allowed to be up this late. They treat it as a kind of festivity—most of them, at least, the ones who have lost no friends to the swan's song. The rest follow our lead demurely, a vacant, disbelieving look on their faces. Is this how I look as well, I wonder? The younger children sing-song as we get ready, their tunes punctuated with shrieks, imitating swans. *Stop that*, I almost say, but I hold myself back. What good would that do, anyway? Let them enjoy themselves.

We gather outside the dorm, teachers and orphans and orphan teachers. We light candles and torches, we bring garlands of flowers and tulle and go down to the shore, carrying the paper swan high above our heads.

There, on the shore, I keep my distance. The other teachers can handle it all well enough, they've done it before. I watch the children dance around the effigy, waiting for the swan song to echo through the night. The surface of the lake is calm, peaceful. For a moment, I think I glimpse Marie's arm laid out on the ground again and my breath catches in my throat, but it's nothing, nothing, just a piece of washed-out driftwood. I brush my fingers through my hair, waiting, sick with anticipation, and then, there it is, the swan's hoarse call piercing the dark like all those years ago. We hear it before we see it, the slender neck curved into an S, the ghostly white wings held high above its back.

The children fall silent all at once, as if on cue. There is no more singing now, no more laughing. They gather behind the paper swan and float it out onto the lake with a slight push.

The swan approaches. He swims around the fake bird in circles. He calls once, twice. We all hold our breath. The swan brushes his neck against his mate. He pauses. In the light of the torches, the fake one's eyes shine, lifeless. Can he tell? He's seen this trick a few times by now, after all. He bends his neck downwards. He glances at us. Is this sorrow in his eyes? He spreads his wings, then folds them behind him again. With a few strong paddles of his feet, he nudges the paper swan away from the shore. For a moment, it seems to me he knows our little ruse but goes along with it anyway, content just to have his sorrow acknowledged. Or tired, perhaps, of all the loss.

Something flutters in my chest. I came back here determined to save or to avenge, somehow; kill the swan, break the spell, walk into the lake myself. Ill-conceived, desperate ideas that probably wouldn't have worked. Meanwhile, the children had already saved themselves. Shouldn't that make me happy? And yet, I'm hollow and unsure, like someone who's been preparing to jump off a cliff all her life, then told there's nowhere to jump from and no reason to. All there's to do now is witness this torment, year after year. Should that satisfy me? Should it make me feel at peace with it all?

The two birds sail away, side by side. Slowly, the paper swan soaks up water. Its delicate feathers droop, little by little, its wings cave in, its neck sags. The air is suddenly very cold; it stings my cheeks, my throat, my eyes.

The prince watches mutely. I think, now, now he'll cry out, now he'll sing one of us to our death, but he doesn't.

When the paper bird finally sinks, the children cheer.

KING SWAN

by Juliana Spink Mills

The swans were back.

Lena watched them float by, three of them, the big one in the middle and the others barely inches from his wing tips. Their reflections rippled across the surface of the glass-still lake so it looked as though there were six swans, three of them oddly distorted. She took a sip of her vitamin shake and pretended it was coffee. She wasn't supposed to drink coffee. No caffeine, no alcohol, no nothing.

It had been a long, long pregnancy.

The tall man had come for her two months before, rapping at the door of the walk-up she shared with six other girls near the blasted ruins of Central Park. "You're beginning to show. The boss lady don't want you seen by no one. She don't want this tied back to her, no way. She has this place, out in the green zone, and she wants you to stay there."

Lena had shrugged, indifferent. After quitting work, she had no money except for what the tall man brought every Monday in a plain, brown envelope. If they wanted her to move, she'd move. It wasn't her baby, anyway.

The baby. Bundle, she'd named it, for the bundle of credits it would bring her at the end of all this mess. A big, fat, untraceable wad of the stuff, as big as the baby inside her belly, big enough to never have to work again.

She'd have enough for anything and anyone. Credits to square her papers and get out of town if she wanted. And maybe she wanted. Maybe she'd buy a place of her own. And she wouldn't buy a flea-ridden walk-up, either, but a nice place like this one. This cottage out here with the swans. She took another sip of her shake and stared out at the lake.

The swans had turned up a week after she'd arrived, on a hot, sultry day somewhere between summer and autumn. Lena had been sunbathing in the small, lakefront garden, exposing her swollen middle to the sun in a too-tight bikini. When she had turned to the side, there were the swans, watching her from the water with their dark, dark eyes.

Mama Karina used to tell tales about King Swan to Lena and the others in the basement sweatshop. There they all were, day in and day out, a ragtag bunch of girls ranging from sixteen to twenty, stuffed underground trying to earn an honest wage. But Lena hadn't minded the life. Not really. Mama Karina was hard but fair. The other girls were like family and it was safer than street work.

Of course, the game she was playing was a lot worse than turning street. Especially after the latest edicts on procreation. If you got caught doing surrogacy, it meant sterilization and the outer rim colonies. Yukon, or maybe even the Arctic, if you were unlucky and got a really harsh judge. If you got sent to the Arctic mining colonies it was as good as a death sentence, she'd heard. No one ever came back to talk about it, but there were plenty of rumors.

At nineteen, she was still officially underage. She didn't reach majority until the Rabbit Year began. She knew that was why she'd been chosen for the gig. But she was still breaking the law, and she wasn't sure being underage counted for much with that lot anyway.

Lena swallowed the rest of her shake, grimacing at the bitter aftertaste. The day was cooling fast, and she was glad for the oversized flannel shirt she'd pulled on. The days here had blurred together until all that really counted were the slowly turning leaves, green to gold and red, and the growing baby kicking away inside.

The swans came closer, and Lena put down the glass and picked up her bread. She waddled over to kneel at the edge of the lake, tearing the bread into small pieces and throwing them to the swans, one by one. The big swan ate first, the voracity at odds with his elegant appearance. Then he backed off and let the others in.

Lena had never seen live swans before she moved to the green zone. The nearest park to the urban tangle of New Manhattan was over in Queens, but that meant crossing the no-mans-land around the riverbanks, and you had to be desperate for that.

"Hello, handsome." The big swan looked at her and bowed his head, as if he would like to answer. His eyes glittered and Lena smiled. She leaned out as far as she dared over the water, Bundle hanging down heavy like the Liberty Bell she'd once seen on a parade float. She held out her hand, but the swan just kept looking, floating slightly out of reach.

Lena hoisted her heavy belly back onto safer ground and sat there in the dirt and grass looking back at him, eye for eye. "You know me," she whispered, "Don't you?"

She watched the lake until the swans left and the sun went down, and it was time to go indoors. The cottage felt very empty. She warmed up one of those ready meals the tall man had left for her and pushed the food around the plate, but she just wasn't hungry. She threw it all away and went to read the gossip mags in bed.

That night it rained, streaks of water that slashed at the windows and rattled the roof. Bundle kicked and squirmed as lightning and thunder ripped the sky to shreds. Lena wrapped her arms around her belly and wished the other girls were there. She wished she was back at Mama Karina's and she had never seen the tall man before, or gone to that white room with the cold tiles and sterile metal table. She wondered once again who the parents were, and why they'd come looking for some down-and-out sweatshop girl to do their carrying for them.

Bundle was a leaden weight, pinning her to the bed.

When she finally fell asleep, she dreamed of King Swan. She danced with him on the polished surface of the lake, their feet leaving a rippled wake in the moonlight. He bent down and wrapped her in his feathered cloak, smiling with his dark, handsome face and ripe lips. And then he pulled her close and kissed her, a sweet, sucking kiss full of passion and promise. The moon shattered into a million pieces of light and King Swan laughed and dragged her down, down into the water, right to the bottom with the waterweed all wet and slimy.

She woke in confusion to a damp bed. She lay blinking in the dark and the storm flashes, and then the pain hit her hard.

Bundle was coming.

The pain streaked across her back and she screamed. Then the ache receded, leaving a dull, throbbing tenderness, and she crawled off the soaked mattress and stumbled swaying to the bathroom.

It was too early! The tall man had promised another month, at least, and then he was coming to take her back to the white room that smelled so clean and weird. And then she'd have her money, all the credits they'd promised her and no street gigs in *her* future, thank you very much.

The pain returned, stronger and harsher this time, and Lena fell to her knees and retched. But King Swan was there too, kissing her brow and holding her tight, telling her it would all be fine, just fine, and hush, trust him now.

Just trust him.

Lena woke to sunbeams through the windowpanes and Bundle in her arms. He was clean and sweet-smelling and so was she, lying soft and cozy on a bed of white feathers all over the floor. Her body was a feather, too, floating free among the dust motes. Through the window, the lake gleamed with sparkling ripples in the morning light. King Swan was waiting for her, his consorts at his side.

She hugged Bundle to her bare chest and walked out of the cottage and to the lake. And then she waded into the water until it covered her head and Bundle's, and dove deep down to the waterweed bottom.

When the tall man came for her later, all he found was an empty cottage and five swans watching from the lake with their glittering, dark eyes.

MOTH'S WING
IN SPIDER'S WEB
by J.E. Bates

Liudan stood on the temple verandah, straining her aging eyes past treetops and foothills. Down in the valley, pillars of smoke curled over fields and villages. Artillery rumbled in the distance.

"My lady," said Sen, emerging from within. "A battalion comes up the road. They'll be here within the hour."

First Ancestor, she thought. *Grant me the strength not to waver.*

"My lady?"

"First Ancestor smiles upon you," she said, greeting him with the same words she used every morning. *Uphold routine in the face of crisis.*

Sen stopped a respectful distance away, face gone pale save for the dark hollows of his eyes. "What shall we *do*, my lady?"

"Do?" She drew a jewel-box from her sleeve, then removed a slender needle of bone from its bed of mulberry silk. With a swift motion, she pricked her index finger, coaxing out a drop of blood before breathing across the crimson bead.

The drop glistened and changed, forming tiny wings and a body, taking the form of a tiny silk moth. The wings, no larger than a spider-leg, beat softly, drying in the wind.

She blew on it: it flew off down the face of the cliff, into the trees. "There's nothing *to* do."

"Order the children and elders into the cellars," Sen said, jaw clenched like a fist. "The rest will fight."

"Courage, fists, and conjuror's tricks—against tanks?"

She stepped closer, touching the knotted muscles beneath his sleeve. "Sen, you are my strength but that is not our way."

⌒

She stood in the courtyard of the temple, hands within her sleeves, greeting each of the Temple's residents by name. They ringed her, stark worry marring placid faces.

"Today shall be a trial, so let us return to first lessons. Who recalls what moved First Ancestor to create poetry?" She smiled at each child present.

One of the boys raised his hand.

That Po, always so quick. "Yes?"

"Moth's wing in spider's web, silver with dew, trembling like first spring."

"That's right. And why did this move First Ancestor to create poetry?" She searched the adults: monks and priests, servants and temple maidens, young and old alike.

At last Sen spoke, voice hoarse: "We are caught in amber but there is no why, and winter brings the wind."

She nodded.

The crowd shifted. A few restless young monks muttered.

"Anyone who wishes to leave may do so," she said. The wind flicked her hair, a touch of smoke in the gusts coming up from the valley now. "You may go, and with my blessing. I shall not blame you for fleeing this storm or striving against it. But if you must abandon your duty in the face of our greatest ordeal, please remove your talismans and break your vows away from this ground."

She held out a hand, waiting for the first talisman. None met her eye or removed their chains. Even Sen bowed his head, though the light in his eyes went out. *Trust a little longer*, she thought. *This too shall pass.*

"Lady Liudan," asked Po. "Can you turn the soldiers into trees?"

She wrapped an arm around the boy. "Would that I had the power, but such strength has vanished from this world. Come, we shall sit in the meadow, have bread and song."

They did as she bid, fetching baskets from the temple and distributing bread and pitchers of water; they brought out the flutes and zithers. Po's mother walked beside her and the boy as they went to sit in the grassy glade outside the temple.

"You've been saving your strength for days," the mother said.

"You are observant," Liudan said. "I shall need all of our strength, in the end."

Within the hour, scouts broached the treeline on the temple's perimeter, crawling through the bramble, their camouflaged faces framed by cut brush tucked in the webbing on their steel helmets. They ducked their heads back down when she waved.

A few minutes later, the high-pitched squeal of tank treads came up the valley trail, accompanied by the deep-throated rumble of a massive diesel engine. A skirmish line of infantrymen burst out of the woods and marched towards them, rifles on their hips, bayonets flashing in the sun.

Her people looked up, songs dying on their lips. She gestured at them to continue: they raggedly resumed.

The soldiers formed around them in a loose circle, guns lowered but ready. Their faces showed a mix of tanned, grizzled veterans and fresh-faced farm boys: as the war dragged on, the Morning Empire had returned to the villages again and again. She recognized some from the better years.

You are Bu the baker's son. I said the words over your grandmother's grave.

A tank rumbled out of the trees, treads churning steel above the grinding engine. A captain commanded from the conning tower atop its hull, an ordinance map like a folded painting in his hand. He leapt down from the tank and bowed correctly to her but kept a wary hand on his holster.

She rose to her feet, offering open palms to the captain and his soldiers. "Welcome to our temple. First Ancestor smiles upon you."

The captain bowed again. "A thousand pardons good lady. Your temple is not on our map."

"We are older than maps." She smiled, hands clasped together.

"We seek rebels. Partisans, hiding in the mountains."

She gestured at her people. "We are but the humble caretakers of an ancient shrine."

The captain consulted with his lieutenants. "May we search the temple?" he asked at last.

"Please do. Here is our treasure," she said, pointing to a blanket where it lay. Folds of silk, gold and silver jewelry, and a few stacks of Imperial scrip weighed down by watches and candelabra. "Take it if you wish, we have nothing else but rations and religious articles."

They did: they secured the goods as Imperial taxes; they searched the temple and a detachment searched her people too, but found only candles and bread, incense and sleeping mats.

She sat back down on the grass, in the ring of her people. The music had broken off again and this time she did not urge them to resume.

The captain spoke on his tank radio, and then approached again. He bowed again, apologetic. "What is the name of this temple, good lady? Who do you serve?"

"We honor all gods and ancestors, but our shrine preserves the memory of a single moment in time."

The captain looked at his lieutenants, who could only shrug.

"Over here," she said, leading across the grass to where an old, gnarled bush, bereft of foliage, stood in a ring of white stones. A spiderweb hung in its branches, dewdrops shimmering in the wind. "Right here but long ago, on a spring morning much like today, First Ancestor beheld a moth's wing in a spider's web. The sight moved him to create the first poetry."

The officers removed their caps respectfully and withdrew. A few soldiers removed their helmets. Bu the Baker's son would not look at her, but after a moment he broke formation and jogged behind the tank. A retching sound came from behind the treads.

Do not tremble, Baker's son. We are caught in amber, that is all.

The young captain apologized then returned to his conning tower to speak with his superiors on the radio again. Back and forth he came, several times, frustration growing in the hardening lines of his jaw. Snatches of conversation came across the meadow, his questions and the static-shrouded hisses of his superiors:

Were they sure? Absolutely sure? There are only religious people here, singing and eating. Yes, absolutely sure, yes, yes—the order still stands.

Finally he hung up the radio and spoke in hushed tones to his lieutenants and sergeants. Some gestured or shook their heads, but at last the huddle broke up, the sergeants making hand signals to their men.

She stood up, clutching Po's shoulders. Her people also rose, clustering around and behind her, praying. "A moment more," she said. "Then this too shall pass."

The soldiers fanned out, facing her group. They held their guns level, the wood-grain stocks cradled against shoulders, gunmetal gray barrels reflecting the shifting clouds.

She stood between Sen and Po, taking their hands in hers. "The cusp of change approaches," she told them softly. "The drop of dew that shall break the web."

The soldiers chambered copper-jacketed rounds, things of perfect beauty themselves: elegant in their uniformity of form and purpose, copper-jacketed shells glittering in the sun. The solders racked back their bolt action rifles with definitive, mechanical clacks. Captain Riku raised his sword, pointing it towards a sky as blue as painted pottery.

Sen's hard fist held hers like a rock.

"Remember," she said. "There is no why, and winter brings the wind."

"Fire!" the captain shouted, bringing his sword down but turning way. Rifles rattled with hot flashes. Puffs of smoke accompanied the brash reek of gunpowder.

Her head rolled back as the bullets touched her; she released what remained of her power, drawing more from the ring of hands, the shrine, the land. *Moth's wing in spider's web*, she thought. *Silver with dew, trembling like first spring.*

The bullets knocked her down, knocked them all down like wheat before a scythe, but instead of blood, moths bloomed from their bodies in the thousands, both large and small, from green and red to blue and purple, iridescent and many-colored, rising into the wind above the awestruck soldiers like a stream of a thousand living flowers; for an instant she lived as an insect did: in a world distilled to scent and chemistry, a thousand lifetimes compacted into a single moment before she vanished in the wind.

Whispers of the massacre and its attendant marvel rippled through the army and reached into every corner of the empire, from the ravaged heartlands to the bomb-scarred capital. Imperial radio and newspapers tried to censor it but amongst a war-weary citizenry it could not be suppressed.

At last the rumor reached the Morning Emperor himself. He demanded the captain's original report: the terse account described how the battalion carried out its orders, executing a reprisal for partisan raids in the prefecture, this time against a nameless temple that had appeared on no map—but when the soldiers carried out their orders the bullets spawned not blood but moths, thousands of them, disappearing into the wind before the bodies and the temple vanished too. Nothing remained but a single stone bearing the characters 'Moth's Wing in Spider's Web.'

Few knew that name anymore, but the Emperor remembered: a temple of that name, lost to the ages, once housed the reliquary of First Ancestor himself. He opened a small, cool tin that accompanied the report, letting a clutch of withered, faded moth wings, crumbling to dust in his fingers—all that remained.

First Ancestor, he thought. *What have we done?*

WALLS OF NIGERIA

by Jeremy Szal

I stare at the twisted remains of Lagos through the visor of my exosuit as I stalk down the hill. Buildings crumble and slide into the sea. Coils of fiery smoke curl up to the sky. So much work, so much craftsmanship. Gone in weeks.

I'm panting as I continue down the hill—with the cooling system broken, I'm swimming in sweat inside this thing. It's gunmetal grey, covering me from sole to scalp and weighing several hundred kilos. If it weren't for the hydraulics built along my spine, moving in it would be impossible. I have to make extra effort to control it now; the suit seems to have a mind of its own. Cancelling my HUD commands, seizing up at random intervals, cutting off my sensory details.

I'm nearing the school I used to attend, years before any of this happened. A few lone palm trees remain, fronds swaying in the sour wind. I remember being in class one stifling Tuesday, me and Tendai trying to sneak out when we first heard we'd captured one of the K'Dasewh. After all these years, we'd finally got an alien.

There are remains of a soldier over by the school. An art mural covers the wall, unfinished words scrawled on blasted brick the colour of red earth. Chalk lies strewn on the ground. Even though his armour has been cracked open, it still pulses with blue bioluminescence. The suit had grown into his flesh like a graft, the metal and matte and wires worming through his dark skin like tendrils. I step over empty coconut shells to check his suit's reading to see when he died. Almost three months ago. He'd been wearing his suit for only two months and he's this far gone.

I've been inside mine for two years.

My skin crawls with the memory of being locked into our suits of armour, laced with alien DNA. They'd dissected these aliens, taken the self-healing and enhanced strength in their biotech and transferred it to us. For a while, it worked.

We didn't know that for the biotech to function and repair us, it needs living tissue. You can't get biomass from nothing. So the suit slowly grew inwards into flesh, tunnelling through open wounds and organs damaged from battle. Fusing into the wearer. The quarantine came around too late.

I wonder if I have any flesh left, if the cables have wrapped around my bones like creepers around a tree. If it's started corroding my brain, trying to take complete control of the suit. Tightening its grip by the day. But I have no way of knowing. And that scares me the most.

Over in the distance, there's a biosphere laid out over the ground—where some of the last human settlements still reside. We're not allowed within five klicks of them for risk of infection. They're still getting refugees from Ghana and Cameroon, but most of them have already been placed on off-world colonies and habitable planets outside the Solar System.

My wife and sons are among them. Ben should be six years old now and Emeka eight, maybe nine.

These are just the last few that have lingered behind on Earth to make sure that no one gets left behind. No one except us.

I log into my commander's channel. It takes me three tries to get it right; the suit attempts to cancel it. But I manage it.

"You still out there, son?" The grizzled face of Commander Somadina pops into my bottom-right vision. "I thought you were dead."

I wish I was. I truly do. "I'm still here."

"I wish I could help. But we can't let any of you Stained inside the sphere. We can't let the biotech virus spread, especially not to the new colony."

My jaws lock and my muscles tighten against my armour. "After everything we did?" I spread my arms, armour plates like fetters around my wrists. "We fought for this city with everything we had."

"And look what happened anyway." He shakes his head. "They sent their entire fleet and destroyed it."

No matter what we did—how hard we fought—it wasn't enough. By the time we'd destroyed the last of their ships, our world was broken.

I crane my neck to look at the sky. Somewhere, out in the giant cosmos of space, is my family. "At least let me talk to my wife one last time. Let me send a message."

"Cannot be done. We can't tell you where the colony is. What if they capture and torture you? Besides, your armour will store the location. All other Stained are in the same position."

I want to scream. I want to laugh like a madman. My throat's filled with concrete and every word feels like it's being fishhooked from my gut. Maybe now the suit has started consuming my throat and vocal cords. Soon I won't be able to speak. "So that's it?"

"I'm so sorry." He can't even look at me. "Goodbye, Kohban."

He cuts the connection. Leaving me here, shackles worming deeper and deeper into my body.

The weight of my armour and of the cosmos pressing down on my shoulders, I stagger to the wall and scoop up some chalk. Hands shaking, I scrawl a message to my friends and family, to the people of Nigeria. I do it quickly, before the armour locks up. Telling them that I miss them—that I'm part of this world now. That the K'Dasewh will never have our planet.

And one day, when my people return to a new, clean Earth, this message will greet them. I hope I'm not here when that happens.

My eyes blur. It could be tears, or could be the suit trying to obscure my vision. I don't think I'll ever know for sure.

OF TALONS AND TEETH

by Brent Baldwin

You should see the things Arana is drawing, Sayid. Elephants with eagle's wings, monkeys with mole's feet. They're amazing. And worrying. When you're released, we'll talk to her about them together, but for now I haven't the heart to tell her to stop. I've enclosed one of her pictures.

⌢

I took one of Arana's drawings to the lab and spliced together some of the gene sequences in the database. The creature is hideous, but it's the only thing that has made her laugh since you were taken. We'll see you next week, yes? I can't wait to show you what she has created.

⌢

You are so strong for us, Sayid. We miss you. I've been taking Arana to work to keep her distracted. Her drawings are getting more detailed, but she still refuses to write to you, saying you'll be home before the letters arrive. I pray five times a day that she's right.

⌢

Grandfather went to the market today, and he didn't come home. Uncle Marwan says he was arrested, but the local police don't have any record of it. I know you can't help us where you are, but if you can think of anyone that can, let us know. It's more likely you'll see him before we do. Tell him we love him, and to be strong. We love you, too.

⌢

It's been a month, Sayid. We need you. Please, if there's anyone else you can think of to plead your case... I know it's not fair of me to ask. I'm sorry. I've spoken to the imam and written to every politician I know, but no one is any help. We haven't forgotten you.

⌢

They're shelling the city. The rebels say it's the government. The radio says it's a few dissidents. We're supposed to stay at home, but we have no home left. If you find this note, come to the lab. We will watch for you.

⌢

Soldiers came to the lab and took Marwan and all the male assistants. I don't know what to do. I will work, I think. It keeps my mind off you for a little while. I... I shouldn't say that. I miss you so much.

⌢

Arana has taken interest in my work. To say she's precocious is to say that the desert is dry. You should see her work the gene splicer. Half the lab's incubators are full of her creations. Little tigers with crocodile mouths, little unicorns with dragon's wings. She calls them her menagerie, but they are the stuff of nightmares.

⌢

You aren't coming home. Neither is Grandfather or Marwan. I know it. You know it. Arana doesn't. I can't bear to tell our baby, Sayid. She needs her father, and what am I supposed to do? Lie to her? She has eyes. She has ears.

⌢

Everyone else has left. Or been taken. It's hard to say. I barely go outside. Arana has had a fever for a week, and I can't get it to come down.

⌢

You won't read these messages. I know that. But it makes me feel better to write them. Arana is still sick. I finally ventured out. I had to.

Most of the soldiers were gone, and I don't think the ones that were left saw me. I went to the university clinic, but there was nothing inside but graffiti and broken glass. The city is dead. We shouldn't stay here, but where else can we go? We cannot leave. Not without you.

⌢

I'm watching my baby die, Sayid. Her skin is on fire. Her heart hammers faster than the machine gun fire outside the lab. Pray for her. Pray for us both.

⌢

Sayid. I love you. Our baby is... gone. There is no heat. No food. Only memories. I cling to the good ones.

I work the gene splicer alone now, trying to do something, anything to take my mind off what I've lost. I am out of protein stock, so I am experimenting on myself. I shouldn't, I know.

I am alive only because I am too much a coward to die.

⌢

Arana's creatures were horrid, nasty things. I am no different. Golden feathers cover my arms. My toes are like talons, fit to crush the world.

⌢

There are soldiers outside. Or rebels. There is no difference any longer. I don't know what they want, but the lab doors no longer lock.

I have nothing to fight them with except my talons and my teeth.

⌢

The lab is nothing but blood and rent flesh. Little of it is mine. My claws are sharp, my wings are strong. I am coming for you, Sayid.

AWAKEN MY BONES
OLD AND NEW

by Beth Cato

The bomb whistles my way. I know because my grandma joined the wind, to warn me in case of this very event, and she's screaming at me now to go, go, go.

Dad's at work. Mom is at the store. It's just me and Buttercup, and I can't linger to say good-bye to anyone else.

"Come on," I tell the cat, and we run.

We live on the edge of the city, where factories exhale fumes that tickle the lungs in awful ways and the countryside still exists in stubborn spurts. I dash into the meadow behind the new car dealership. Spring grass lashes my knees with tears.

"I know," I tell the grass. It hears the missile coming, too. Birds argue in the trees about where to go and what to do, not unlike humans. Birds are just a different sort of people, really.

Fear shakes me like I'm cold. The birds, the people, the cats, the grass. They're all depending on me, but can I really do this?

Buttercup bounces ahead of me, her tail an orange plume. "I hear your heartbeat from here."

"I'm scared." And I really want to keep on being a kid. Hanging out with my dad, absorbing his infectious passion for baseball, the tenderness in how he ruffles my hair. Learning from my mom, who didn't inherit the ancientness from grandma like I did, but is the smartest person I know.

I want to stay in this city. It's not perfect, but it's home. I could grow up here, being kinda-sorta normal, living out my body's years, like Grandma did.

"All the world is scared, with reason," Buttercup says. One of her ears flicks, and then I hear the chaos of a city that knows death screams its way. I can see the domino effect that spirals out from here, the tit-for-tat retaliation determined to send us into deep winter.

For some reason, this calms me. I'm not alone in my terror. I know I must stop the chain reaction at the start.

I come to the ditch. I find four stones smoothed by the stroke of water. On the far bank, the spiders have already heeded Grandma's warning and gathered at the span between two fence posts. In a mass of hundreds, spiders weave a pattern ancient and new, flexible and strong.

Fear strikes me again. "I'm just eleven, I want to live out this life," I whisper, only to be chastised with a lash of wind. I am far, far older in truth, though most of what I remember is in the fog of dreams.

What I do remember, with the clarity of a rain-washed sky, is death, and that it must be stopped.

I raise my arms. Buttercup bellows out a yowl that expands as the wind carries it around the world. The full planet falls silent and still.

Into the quietude, I sing verse that makes snakes sigh and clouds curdle, a melody that awakens stones and inspires rainbows. The wind joins me again with all of a hurricane's bluster. Power leaches from corpses I once wore, to surge into my young brain with a million flickering images of love and loss and the promise of humanity. A promise that could not be lost today.

Buttercup rubs against my leg, a sweet gesture of farewell, and then I surge toward the heavens. The woven net flies to my hands. I fling the stones to the net's four corners, to weight it with all the heft of boulders. Clouds swipe tears from my cheeks as I rise higher, higher. Land curves behind me, the ocean an endless sprawl. Grandma hugs me, best as she can from within the wind, and I mourn the death of her human body and miss how she used to smile and the way she always smelled like baby powder.

But we're far more than frail human bodies. We're gods and guardians, part and parcel of everything on this world. And we have jobs to do, tasks more awful than algebra and diagramming.

I meet the missile.

I throw the net. It stretches against the force of modern science so tidily sheathed in sleek metal, but I hold the web tight. I'm an eleven-year-old girl. I'm strong. The wind braces me as I swing the missile around and around, and just like when I play softball, I know where to throw. I aim for a distant island already decimated by such bombs.

I fling myself home as my awareness of the ancient fades.

I awaken in an impact crater. I lift my head to desperate meows that grow closer with every bound, then Buttercup is there, purring and writhing against me. Mom follows, scrambling into the pit. She may not possess an old soul, but she's a mom, and powerful in her own right.

The wind taps my ears. A new missile has screamed to life, from our shore. It threatens to streak across the sea, retaliation for a strike that never met its target.

I stand. I must act now, though it'll take all that I have. Already, the spiders rally anew.

I don't want to go. I don't. Dad bought tickets for a baseball game next Saturday. He promised to get me ice cream.

"You always have a choice," yowls Buttercup.

"Do I really?" I ask. "How many will die when that bomb strikes? How many more counter-attacks will that horror inspire?"

I waver in place, my young body suddenly heavy with anger, love, grief, frustration. But I have to go. I have to defy gravity and mortality again.

"We love you. Come home, however you can," Mom chokes out. She's the wind's daughter. She knows what this will cost me.

"And I love you," I say, to her, my cat, and all the world. I will return home, somehow, perhaps joining Grandma for a time before I settle again into newborn cartilage and bone.

KQ'

by Nicole Givens Kurtz

A tickling softness brushed Yazhi's fingertips as her mother's blanket slid out of her hands. Her mother folded it in a quick fashion before picking up another one. The frenzied actions were being repeated all over the village. An ochre glow rimmed the village. The entire land seemed to have captured the sun in its mouth and burped up flames. As the fire crawled across the mesa, it chewed up everything in its path. Bold and brave, it fought back the cold darkness. The forces jumped onto the edge of their lands and crept ever closer.

The smoke rose into the sky and thickened with each passing moment. Wails, hurried voices, and the sharp tones of the villagers echoed amongst the ash-thick air. They had to push on, for Black God had erupted here, in this place—their place. It meant nothing for him to escape the confines of their Hogan, and began to ravage the land, turning the tumbleweeds, cacti, and man into its food. Terror shook Yazhi, for she'd never seen anything like this before.

This was her first contact with Black God. The son of a comet and fire, Black God was lord of kq', fire. Tales told by her grandfather, a powerful medicine man, spoke of Black God's cowardice and transformative powers.

How could they believe Black God was helpless when he chewed the landscape and ravished all in his path? With eyes wide, Yazhi clutched her mother's dress with mounting fear. The soft fur of her mother's blanket offered small comfort. It hung from her shoulders as she bent down to retrieve a fallen basket.

Yazhi shut her eyes and turned her face into the fur.

"What ails her?" her father demanded, his voice rough from the smoke.

"Black God's power is displayed this night. It is Yazhi's first time in his presence." Her mother coughed. "It comes closer."

Her father growled. When Yazhi looked at him, she saw him shake his head in mounting disappointment, but whether that was for the situation or her actions, she didn't know.

"Here. Take these."

Her mother gave Yazhi a small smile, and pressed items into her hands. Bits of pottery filled with grain, oil, and turquoise. She followed her mother's glance to the semi-circle of fire, kq', that leapt up and vanished into the billowing sky. At the same time, kq' managed to remain on the ground. As if angered, it crackled and popped in its efforts to speak to them, even as it consumed all in its path. Her people had to leave before they too became food for the kq's belly.

She had never before seen it so wild and untamed.

Yazhi spoke soft against the thick air. "What do you want?"

The maize lay collected in hand-woven baskets, ready for the journey to the neighboring village. As the elders told of the first people, First Woman and First Man were joined forever by this world to those that had come before them. The different types of maize represented the various people who eventually became the Dine'. The flickering called to Yazhi to come, to touch, and to feel its power.

Entranced, she headed toward it.

Black God's kq'. It moved across the mesa, old and slow like the god himself, but then fast and furious. She pictured herself standing tall in its orange-yellow glow as First Woman once did in the yellow world, when she first met Black God.

Like Yazhi tonight.

Somehow she'd walked closer to the kq' than to her home. Mesmerized, she watched it dance for her and she reached out her hand to join in its joy. Now that she had come closer, it did not seem so bad.

"Ow!" She yelped as flames bit her. She rubbed the angry spot on her hand.

Her mother stuck her head out of the Hogan's entrance. "Yazhi?"

Yazhi waved. "Here!"

Her mother's face became alarmed. "Yazhi! Get away from that fire!"

"But...."

"Now! Come closer to me, beside the house." She waited until Yazhi had started back toward the Hogan, but the clatter and clang from inside the dwelling drew her attention away.

All around the family Hogan, people trekked back and forth between their homes, mules, and horses. Yazhi's mother continued to bring out items and tie them onto the family's own pack animals.

Once her mother had disappeared back into the Hogan, Yazhi turned back to the fire. She couldn't take her eyes away from its newfound display of magic. The growing kq' battled back the gloom, a fierce and greedy warrior. She found herself back at the edge of the blaze, within arm's reach once more.

Moving closer to her village, the kq' gobbled everything in its path. Its power grew as it fed. When it appeared to be winning the eternal fight, it reached higher to the dark sky as if summoning its lord.

Yazhi stumbled backward. Her items spilled to the earth. The heat licked at her as if finding her delicious. She searched behind for her mother or someone, but there was only the constant motion of people on the move.

These weren't the only movements in the night.

Yazhi watched as the moon overhead folded in to the gathering dark, and stepped down onto the ground in front of her. Obediently the fire withdrew, but only from the place of darkness, where he stood. It was Black God! She couldn't mistake him. His mouth was a full moon, and a crescent moon had been etched into his forehead. Elderly and mysterious, his smile frightened her.

The kq' leapt around excitedly, like children did when their parents came home.

"Come into my embrace, little one," Black God encouraged.

"Why?" Yazhi wanted to run, but she couldn't get her feet to obey. Her mouth struggled to form words. The fact that she'd managed to ask the one question surprised her.

"Because I demand it." He did not smile now. His face was hidden in shadow. Coward.

The whims of gods had become legendary. Yazhi looked around, but no one else seemed to notice Black God towering into the heavens.

She swallowed her fear and tried to look up into his face. Where did he want to take her? She didn't want to leave her family. It had been his doing that her people had to leave this settlement. Yazhi knew her family, like other Dine', had grown tired of being uprooted, first by the white men, and now this.

So, she steeled her strength and pooled her courage. First Woman did not shy away from this lazy god, who let his offspring do his work for him. Neither would she. He could demand whatever he wanted, but she had some demands of her own.

"No." Yazhi tossed her plaits over her shoulder. With her hands on her narrow hips she glared at him, but only a moment before looking away.

"No?" He rumbled when he spoke and the sky shook.

For a god of kq', he made her very cold.

Someone cried out and she looked across to the many people streaming across the horizon. Sheep, mules, and people displaced by Black God's appetite—or whim.

Yazhi turned back to Black God. "I will come with you, but you must stop destroying the village."

"I will destroy this valley, the mesa, and your village and you will come with me." He waved his hand and the raging ochre grew higher.

"I am the granddaughter of Chief Manuelito! You will not threaten me or my people!"

She stamped her foot. Inside, a magic warmth spread through her, filling her with light that poured from her fingertips. Her heart thundered in her chest as she directed them into the eyes of Black God, who screamed in agony.

He could burn her to ash where she stood! That knowledge terrified her. But all the pent-up disappointment, rage, and confidence of youth ignited her own inner kq'.

Besides, Yazhi reasoned, Black God had already devoured much of the land surrounding her village, if not the homes themselves.

"Yazhi?" Her mother poked her head out of the Hogan's doorway. Her dark hair blew on the breeze, but it failed to hide the fear on her face. "Come!"

When Yazhi turned back to look at Black God, he had vanished. His chuckling echoed on the wind. The moon hung in its full glory in the heavens above, and all appeared as it had been before.

Yazhi checked her hands. They seemed ordinary. No light. No scars. Nothing.

"We are leaving!" her father called as he climbed on the horse. He waved his family to him, and Yazhi raced to join them. He sounded tired, but strength showed in his movements. He would endure. Their people would endure, as they have forever, for the Dine'.

The air tasted like ash, smoke, and dirt. Yazhi too smelled of smoke, and her moccasins were covered in soot. She glanced once more at the village, then back to the kq'. She'd done what she could to save her village, but the flames continued to advance.

Her efforts had been in vain.

"Look! The fires are changing!" Her mother pointed to the orange glow that winked out near the first set of Hogans. It looked as if stronger kq' had taken hold on the western edge of the lands, closer to the canyons—away from their village.

Black God was turning his glowing offspring. Like a starving sheep, the kq' demonstrated its powerful appetite, consuming everything in its path. But as it continued its dance with the wind, it moved away from the village.

Her mother hugged Yazhi to her as her father joined them. They watched the darkness and the illumination of the kq' engaged in battle.

Yazhi rested her head on her mother's shoulder. "Do we still have to leave?"

"No, little one. We do not." Her mother kissed her forehead. "We do have to bring everything back into our home."

Yazhi groaned, and both her parents laughed.

"Watch the kq', Yazhi, as it continues its dance with its partner, the wind," her mother encouraged.

Yazhi looked out to the destroyed lands. She'd never seen anything so beautiful, and so harsh before.

She hoped she never would again.

THE SCORCHING

by Dan Rabarts

She stands on the ridge, one hand pressed to her belly, and the tears cut lines in the ash on her cheeks. There is blood on her legs and a burning inside. Nothing can live in this place. Not anymore. So she can spare a moment to grieve, scanning the blackened skyline. It's a long time since she's seen the hills this blasted. There'd been a bushfire, back when she was no higher than her nana's knee, the horizon reduced to rills of black under the hazing sky. The wind blew away the ash to leave the earth lifeless grey, and the summer sun had withered what was left to tinder and dust.

The bush had never come back.

She remembers scrub, after that, and grass, and gorse, and thistle. Dust and dry earth, tall thin weeds with small yellow flowers that smelled of urine. Sun, and the dirge of wind through twisted branches, too many months without so much as a whisper of rain, the west wind rasping over this corpse of earth day after night after day.

There is power, then, in death.

So she wipes the blood from her legs, and she scrapes in the dirt with bleeding fingers, her nails breaking, and there she lays the small warmth. There, a fragment of life now growing cold, in a lifeless land growing ever hotter. It shall not be for nothing. Not like before.

She crushes the dried seeds, and grinds last year's herb leaves, and wets the powder with the blood of her loss, and she smears this upon her chin and her cheeks and her breast, and she walks along the ridge and bares herself to the sky, and wills the rain to come. She speaks the ancient words to the bleak horizon, words from her mother's lips, from her grandmother's. Words to persecute the killing sun and bring cool falls of rain.

The sky stares back, blue and blind and unforgiving.

So she walks along the rocky coast, and remembers the lover who went into those waves and never came back. She piles high the crackling black strands of seaweed on crosshatchings of sunbaked driftwood, and she collects the many shells that gather and scatter upon the wavewracked rocks, and spreads them through the pyre before she strikes stone to stone and watches the fire rise.

The words she now speaks were her father's, her grandfather's, low growls like the grind of rocks in the waves, of coals in the flame. She drags burning branches from the fire, douses them in the salting swell, and smears her arms and belly in wet ash. She shouts to the hills, and the sea, and the sky, until the blood on her face is streaked with salt, and still the barren blue will not cry for her.

Finally, she knows that even the sacrifice which came from within her was not enough. So she delves into the sandy caves at the water's edge, that final place where earth and sea and time collide to wear each other down, and there in the waves she takes the sharp-edged seashells and she cuts her hair, scrapes it ragged from her head, and she drags the razor's edge down her arms, her legs, slices open her feet and her hands and lets the sand and the sea soak up her offerings. She has no words for this.

The waves thunder and the shifting rocks mock her with their cackling, and the spray drips tremulous from her quivering lips, paling pink as it trickles into the sand. But still the sky does not relent. Instead, the sun scours all that is left, and in the damp cool of her caves she has not the tears to water the earth. The time for supplication is over. She knows the taste of defeat.

Upon the ridge, staggering and bloody, she turns to gaze on the rolling waves of dirt that spill towards the ocean, sees shadows and devils of dust swirl across the blasted earth. Her words are no longer those of ancestors past, but simply her own. "Why?" she whispers, her voice the brittle crack of dead branches in the sun.

Because we are tired of giving, whisper land, sea and sky in their many-fathomed voice.

She knows she's losing her mind; that she's weak from loss of blood, from too many long days with too little food, too little water, and the possibility that some sickness burns through her. But she does not doubt the truth of the words.

"But you are life. Without you, we are nothing." She thinks of the herbs and the seashells, crushed and burned and twisted into magic; of the goats, their leavings fuelling her fires as their skins cloak her back, their flesh filling the empty places inside her. Of the bush and all its life, now gone and gone, stripped away.

We will always be something, sooth the trio of voices. *You are nothing.*

It hits her then, like a breaking wave. What she knew before was an illusion, all that love and loss merely a waking dream, an eyeblink distraction. She clings too tightly to things she could never have, and fights too hard against the fear and the pain of everything else. She could be dried, and ground, and know the succour of sunrise to sunset, the swell of spring tides and the fresh brisk taste of summer rain, the aching howl of October gales. She could be burned to ash to scatter on the earth and sea and sky. She could become all these things, for which there are no words and never can be, only the groans of an animal laid out to die.

In her wake, the blood from her feet dries to dust and blows behind her like pale scarlet phantoms. She comes to the place where the bones of her ancestors rest; those of their homes; of the sheep and goats and fish that breathed of sky and fed on earth and sea. Where she so gently laid the life that grew, and died, inside her. Where memories never wither and break apart on the rasping wind.

With hammered metal tools she turns the black earth until the embers give up their secrets, to stare baleful and smouldering at the sky, and with her breath she coaxes them to a scorching blaze.

You cannot burn us.

She piles the flames ever higher, the smoke darkening the sky and casting a pall across the sea. Timber from the houses she throws upon the pyre, and the dry piled remains of long-dead orchard trees, and the bleached bones of the cloven-hoofed, and tangles of old seaweed, and violent leap the sparks.

She has wailed the words of her mother, barked the curses of her father, words of pain, bloody like childbirth, red and raw and desperate and screaming, and all her invective has come to naught. She is done with words. Words alone cannot challenge the voice of dust and wave and wind. She digs again, and finds what she is looking for, down among the dirt and the dead. So cold, so small she can clutch it to her breast in the span of her two hands.

A spark settles on the house, her grandmother's house, and thus the conflagration swells, encircles her like a womb of death, a crucible in which to be melted and reformed. It sears her skin.

You are no phoenix. You will not rise from the ashes.

All the old empty houses are burning now, their occupants long gone, she alone to watch the ancestral homes die.

We are done with your ways, speak land, sea, sky, as if there is need for explanation. *Once you are gone, we will start again.*

Her voice, when it returns to her, is cracked like hot ash, rough as smoke. "No," she rasps, "You would curse me with barrenness eternal, but I will be one with the earth, where my love lies, and with the sea, where my lost heart wanders." She places one hand over her empty womb, the other holding the tiny dead thing, the tiny loved thing, the tiny thing that she never knew, tight to her heart. She steps toward the blaze, her skin growing dry and brittle.

Earthseasky rumbles, as if to protest.

There is, after all, a power in death.

She steps forward. The fires taste her tears. Though her lip trembles, she will not bow.

The rumble rises to thunder. Behind the sucking heat of the flames, a cool wind. From sudden clouds, fat wet rain hisses around her. On the shore, waves break upon the rocks in futile rage, as smoke boils into the sky and the flames leap high.

Still she steps forward.

So we relent, growls Earthseasky, as the rain rises to a hammering dirge. *Step back.*

The fire licks at the crusted blood on her legs, and her bone-dry linens spark and catch. She hugs her child to her chest. "No," she whispers, like cool rain gurgling between mossy stones. She can't step back. She can never step back. There is nowhere left to step back to. "Why, when I can join you, and haunt you forever?"

The flames rise. The wind carries the ashes into the sky, to fall with the rain, and soak the barren earth.

DARK THE SKY, RUST THE EARTH

by Hal Y. Zhang

The summer rain halts as quickly as it began. He emerges beneath the tree canopy, shakes his feathers, drinks from the renewed pond. Liquid netal, sharp and unfamiliar. He has no sense of memory or self, and does not know he has been here most his life. Does not know he grew from an airborne mote from the other side of the world, carried aloft on a leaf.

Flies radiate in every direction as he uncurves his body, eyeing quick flitting shadows in the water. In this otherwise unremarkable moment, the colors of the world invert for one blink. His breath stops. There is something...a beat beneath his feet, a quickening in his pulse. His legs thrust against the earth as he walks around, looking for a spot to anchor his ears, but the ground is too hard, all pale impassable rock.

Neck tweaking in thought, he approaches the water where two long dark legs and feathers float against silver light. He wades in deeper and deeper to push his legs into the cool bank, sand swirling up to dispel the picture. Ah, now he can hear.

It must be her. The envelope of the waveform is her name, the changes in frequency her message. A long and complex signal, but it says only one thing.

Come. Come. Come.

He has never heard it before, but no—that is untrue. She is his destiny and he knows, for it is written in his bones and features and very being. He must go now, go and find her.

His wings spread, beat twice and he is aloft, the pond disappearing below into insignificance as he rides the urgent air. Up here above the clouds he can see the curve of the world, and somehow he knows the destination is still beyond the edge. When he feels he is merely riding on the wind and can give no more of his own power, he settles down to earth, drinks water and life, inserts his feet into the ground to hear her rhythmic song.

At every watering hole others join him on the journey. Soon there are enough black lines to blot out the sun. Their wings stroke in synchrony, driven by the message that now pulses in their blood even when airborne. *Come.* When he drinks he sees a panoply of figures in the water: swirls of feathers, long legs. Black on black on black.

Some of his brethren bring offerings to her, small pebbles and creatures in their proboscises. It is an instinctive urge in all of them. He searches for a suitable gift at each watering hole, desiring something permanent, unique—but how can his gift be different when there is more black than blue sky?

Finally he picks a single small flower, already beginning to droop, and takes flight. As his vision fills with white threads woven in black he knows he no longer needs to leave the sky, for the pulse is so strong it carries *them* now, air and water and fuel. Her drum beats their hearts and wings.

As storm clouds roll in, he senses a change in the formation but does not know why. The message thrums as it veers downwards, vertical ebbs and flows piercing his heart. Suddenly it disappears entirely: he collapses, free-falling into the eye of the storm. All around him they fold their wings and dive sharply, a dark lightning strike hurling toward the earth. Here she lies, waiting.

He plummets with the others, lost in the absence of her voice. Between wings and legs he glimpses yellow sand. Somehow they know she is buried underground, can almost see the shape of her, long like the skeleton of an ancient whale. With his last remaining strength he folds himself into a single dimension, a sharp black ray aiming true.

The world inverts from light to dark—or is it dark to light—and he knows he is home. He can see her now, can only see her. Her enormous structure borne of innumerable sharp black lines, stacked in a dizzying trellis that repeats itself as he swoops ever closer.

These are the remnants of those who have gone before him, dark rust red, feathers and legs disintegrating before his eyes, flesh and blood splitting, reforming into energy, into the message. This is where he came from, tiny stick splitting off of the mother. His end and beginning.

He dissolves, and suddenly he is everything: the voice, the mother, the sons. His wings and legs become his descendants, the flower his destiny. Bursting forth into spores, he floats on the wind with the petals until falling onto earth and water to begin anew.